I0772583

WE WENT
FOR A
WALK

Cover & Chapter Art By Ruben Ramires

Table of Contents

| Proem: Somewhere in August | 1

1 | Dutch | 11

2 | Rivs | 18

3 | Friend Match | 25

4 | Baby Steps | 44

5 | Best Fries & No Lies | 58

6 | Your Turn | 72

7 | Let's Walk | 100

8 | Unamious Swinging | 109

9 | Rewound Compasses | 122

10 | The Planning of Plans | 147

| Postlude: The Next Day in October | 166

Content Warning

There's an invisible relationship between an author and a reader. And as the said author, I do not wish for the challenges and hardships of our realities to be hidden and unrepresented. But I want to address them here for those who may not be comfortable with these topics.

Please carefully read the following content warning subjects. If one or more is unsettling to you, please put yourself and your self-care first.

|| Anxiety || Bullying || Cancer || Death of Parent || Eating disorder ||

There's a special place in my wee author heart, my readers, which is why this page is so very important. No matter where you are in life, please know that your boundaries, trials, experiences, and self-care are of the utmost importance. There is always a place for you in this world; you deserve your spot on this beautiful planet. Take care of yourself and show kindness, and I sincerely hope you enjoy this story.

-B.A. McRae

Proem

Somewhere in August

Rivers was born on August 10th, right on the dot at 11 o clock. She screamed once, intensive and loud, already demanding immediate attention. Ironically after receiving it, she subconsciously presumed that it was perhaps not for her.

She was born to a busily ambitious Mother, an absent-minded Father who was also absent in presence, and what she would soon see to be a hovering older sister. In her defense, she does have four more years of experience in this world than Rivers. And while on the subject, she was rarely called Rivers, and she preferred her alternative- Rivs.

Rivs was unapologetically preoccupied in her mind, even from infancy. There just seemed to be more pressing and far more exciting matters to meddle in inside her head. Suggestions of alternate ways of life, nonsensical human habits, and her favorite continuous fictional stories that she would pick up in moments of boredom or escape. Much like the action of picking up a book from a coffee table.

Rivs was born precisely as predicted, by the Doctors, by her mother's psychically claiming acquaintance, and by her mother's profoundly rooted intuition. She was right on time.

Dutch was born on August 15th, precisely at 11 o clock. The Doctor seemed alarmed that the baby had hardly gasped when he was yanked out, and he was indeed *yanked* by the fact it was an emergency c-section from a business-oriented surrogate. Who was less than thrilled that her pregnancy, which she referred to as an agreed-upon business plan, was way behind schedule.

He was born to ecstatically patient parents. Fathers who had been proper names on a lengthy list for numerous lagging years, waiting for their chance to have a family. Once they held Dutch in their arms, he was hardly out of their reach physically and emotionally, even as a young adult.

Dutch tried not to let his mind wander too far; sometimes, it felt like ages to reel it back in, only to get carried away again. He thought he had enough going on in the present then to let far-fetched possibilities consume his current energy.

Dutch was supposed to be born five days earlier, but from out of his control, he was late. These two souls were *supposed* to be born on the same day, but they were *not* meant to cross paths until later in their lives.

Lives that would be marked with events of loss and random moments faded into barely recalled memories yet would shape their personalities and beliefs. The two would also create a hidden collection of built-up emotions they had no intentions of sharing the stock—only the unaccompanied air floating about their homes at night.

Dutch and Rivers, passive and stubborn, were meant to meet at a time in their lives when they both would be oblivious to the obvious help and encouragement they desperately needed. To their unseen convenience, they were each other's destined prescriptions for this rough patch of time.

Destiny is often seen as dramatic, and that it may be to some degree, but more importantly, it surges with a powerful air of promise. A promise that *these things happen for a reason* actually has a point, that destiny never fails to fulfill what it is written to do. The misconception is destiny gets tangled up with words like forever, everlasting, something romantic, and once again dramatic. But on occasion, on this particular occasion, destiny was only meant to be for 24 hours.

When Dutch came into the world unwillingly late, he was seeded with a compulsive obsession for punctuality. For goodness sake, the very first room he ever occupied was riddled with tension and uneasiness from his tardiness. And only when he was finally placed in the arms of his fathers would he feel the much-needed comfort of acceptance and security. For there was a scheduled time for his fathers to meet him, and Dutch was brought to them right on time.

If Dutch was even a minute off, he felt thrown from the very course of his existence for days. And while off the path, his mind would hitchhike along with it and become so entangled in a jumble of problems and issues he wasn't even fully aware he was dealing with. Or shall we say, apparently, not dealing with. He always tried his best to remain on track for his sanity and obsessive loyalty to schedules and time.

He had harbored several things deep within the marina of his mental health. Dutch saw mirrors and looked at them differently than most others, the fortunate ones. Avoiding them was his main ploy, but when given no other choice or glanced at by accident, he is drawn into a false reflection. His eyes become fixated, even though he would want nothing more than to tear them away. His muscles, hardly seen to the naked eye, would become paralyzed in the mirror's presence until the vicious ridicule had dictated and manipulated his vulnerable mind.

Dutch stands at 5'10 and weighs about 120 lbs. so far, the most he has ever weighed. He is obviously a slender lad, but the mirror plays the cruel trick of distorting his appearance into a figure he can hardly look at without crying or becoming so internally upset he shuts down. There was a time when Dutch never even really thought about his physical appearance, at least not in a negative way, but due to the tidal waves of intoxicating masculinity surrounding him by horrid peers that were dealing with their own closeted struggles, he developed untreated body dysmorphia, along with an eating disorder.

Unlike Rivs, who was born precisely when was predicted, it was after that transition from scream to silence that she would continue to be as unpredictable and untraditional as possible.

The more she pulled from what people expected of her, the more her rebellion felt like the core of her identity. Although in her mind, she didn't label herself as a rebel. That would be horrendously counterproductive because she was more than positive if the world around her were given a chance to slap a label on her, as silly humans impulsively do, it would be that 5-letter word. Rivs remained as labelless as possible, maybe to confuse people, which amused her, and to press on with the philosophy she created for herself. Within the gardens of her mind laid the invasively radical roots that if she remained this perplexing, almost off-putting person, people would eventually catch the vibe and leave her be. So she could continue her life's endeavors without the unnecessary noise of mundane nonsense. Social statuses, grossly romanticized patriarchal toxicity, and she particularly detested forced knowledge. Basic knowledge she understood, knowing how to add and subtract numbers comes in handy but learning falsely painted 'history' made her cherry Kool-Aid-stained veins boil with a rage her mother most certainly implemented in her, but she willingly decided to carry out on her own principals of equality. Throughout her middle and high school career, she was known for 3 things:

1.   Impromptu, but impressively accurately informative, History class protest speeches. To which she would take her punishment of sitting in detention.

2.   Her appointed nickname Rivvie Commie.

3.   The messenger bag that went everywhere with her, scrawled with Sharpie-bled swear words written in Icelandic.

Some people get stuck in their ways due to fear of the unknown outside their comfort zone, stubbornness, or lack of acknowledgment of their unhealthy habits. But for Rivs, she clearly saw her way of living; how different it was from others, how people judged her absurdity and disturbing quirkiness, and by all the gravity and logic in the universe, she flipped the bird and lived out intentionally. What made a person such a devoted radical? Ironically, she was the most closed open-minded person you would ever encounter.

1

Dutch

Oranges, reds, yellows, and even a few lucky shades of green were graciously decorating the city's trees. They were fitted to the nines with festive generosity in their genetically assigned colors. They even sprouted out into the knitted sweaters that bounced in their step along the sidewalks, wool hats that hustled into coffee shops on the corner and embellished otherwise bare doors with warmly welcomed greetings of thankfulness and harvest-like activities. Even the very presence of its existence struck inspiration in corporations to offer discounts of 25% during the celebratory season.

It's the first day of October. Fall has hastily swept up under my feet as it always does, and isn't it interesting that a single day can mean nothing or everything to a single person?

Think about that, a day that resembles nothing more than the huff and puff of catching up on household chores could be the anniversary date of someone's conquered worst fear (commitment, it's a wedding anniversary)!

In any case, nothing particularly noteworthy has happened to me on this day in the history of my life. At least not that I can remember. Maybe at one point, something happened, and I swore I'd never forget it, but as time has come to unfold, I guess it faded into memory dust and blew off the shelf to make way for new memories I'll vow to *never forget*. If I think about that too much, memories and the frustration of not remembering every single one, I'll start to get sad. So, moving on.

Today I actually have a monumental memory in the works. It's my first official day on the job. My training has been completed, and I'm still shocked that I was chosen out of all the applicants for this position. I now work for Lend a Friend, a fairly new nonprofit that spans most of the major cities in the U.S. and is even making its way to Europe (first stop, London!).

Lend a Friend is a service for humanity; when loved ones are too far away, or unable to connect with someone due to a broken relationship, they may send a request to Lend a Friend. Essentially, this is how the service's system works:

A concerned person submits a Comfort Connection Request (C.C.R.) to Lend a Friend (L.A.F.). This is usually requested for a day that is hard for the requested individual or the individual is currently going through an awful lot, and the requestor fears for their wellbeing and cannot be there to comfort them.

After a background check is done on the requester and their associated individual to ensure there are no current or pending restraining orders, criminal charges, or any other illegal concerns, the C.C.R. will be sent through to find a Friend Match.

Friend Matches are a part of the duty of a trained and employed Empath of L.A.F. The employed Empaths are continuously priming their comfort, listening, and creative problem-solving skills with provided workshops throughout the L.A.F. While waiting to be assigned a Friend Match, Empaths can be found providing undivided attention and intentional help through the international Empath phone/video call line.

Once the friend match is made, they are given a telegram (of sorts) that's been submitted by the requester that has the details of their assigned C.C.R. This contains the time requirements of the visit, where they should go to see the individual, and what message to give the individual upon meeting them to start the C.C.R.

I've been intensely training for this highly competitive position for two weeks. I was even told on several occasions that I'm a natural. Although, I'm not sure if that was said out of their own trained empathy or if they were indeed genuine compliments on my emotional intelligence. Either way, after I had passed all of the required training material and had an outstanding evaluation, I was appropriately anointed as an official L.A.F. Empath and given my very first C.C.R.

For me, this was a huge deal, an honor even. Maybe this could be my new escape from my own weighted-down mind. A way to give back, to help someone else.

The C.C.R. instructions and inscriptions were always printed on this iconic tangerine-colored paper that L.A.F. used for every promotional and professional piece of merchandise and stationery. Mine read the following:

Comfort Connection Request: Rivers Talantirt, 25

Time requirement: 24 hours

Location: 326 S 12th St., Apartment 23

Message upon arrival: "Rivs, please don't close your door this is important. I am worried about you. I don't want you to be alone, at least not for this day. Please do this for me; I know that will make you not want to do it but just, surprise me, okay? Love, Mom."

2

Rivs

This day sucks—point blank. In the grand scheme of things, it really is just a day, but it's batshit crazy how a single shitty day can drum up such a heavy-handed tone for what seems to be an eternity. Life will never stop being crazy; we just have to keep up.

Four years ago, on this day, I experienced a rip in the fabric of my life's quilt. A colorful, meaningful, and inspiring square was damaged, torn, and cut away. This led my other squares of fabric in this metaphorical quilt to tatter or detach themselves from the oddly vibrant yet washed-out pattern of a quilt that represents me. I dress it up to be all whimsically melodramatic, but really, it's just depressing as hell. I felt like I was losing myself, without trying, and with complete fear. And so, I conjured survival in my own crafty way. Isolation became my tactic.

When I used to be alone, and I mean *entirely* alone, I felt the side effects of what people typically feel: anxious, lonely, sad, uneasy, bored. But I pushed myself to keep experimenting with this newfound isolation; I combined it with my gifts of creativity, I tossed in some online side businesses of freelancing and digital arts, and most importantly, I carved out time for the vast world of stories inside my mind. To keep from going stir-crazy, which is not a part of the tactic, I have an email pen pal who is undergoing the exact lifestyle change. We know each other by the names of our favorite musical artists; they're Iggy Pop, and I am Cat Stevens. Besides that, I have been experiencing the reality of being alone.

Alone, I can freely speak and act out any scene that comes to mind so I can then write it perfectly from the character's perspective. Alone, I have the power to control the vibe of the room and the entire mood for the day. Alone, I may be whoever I feel like being that day; and in time, I found that on most days, I didn't mind just being still and being whatever mess of organisms I am.

Then there are days when I completely hate everything I have built, but I mark those as glitch days.

Some may turn to substances when they feel bored or need some numbing, but I've never touched or indulged in beer, wine, liquor, weed, Adderall, sex, or other sexual matters. Witnessing the effect it had on people, or rather the hold it had, I decided from a young age that I wasn't going to let my creativity be touched by anything that could alter the imaginative world that has established itself in the hallways of my brain.

I've tried explaining this when I'm offered a drink, a hit, or hit on, and I don't expect for it to be understood I would just think it would be respected. Oh well.

We do all have our vices, though. No matter who we are, they just look different. And mine is Cherry Kool-Aid.

When I mentioned my gifts, I'm referring to what my mom would tell me. From as early as I can remember, which is an annoying thing to say because who can even directly pinpoint that statement but whatever, my mom told me I held these wonderous gifts for creativity. Drawing, painting, writing, storytelling, imagining, and feeling. I didn't hold much weight to what she said until my pieces started gaining attention from fascinated local artists, which extended to local galleries, then leaked itself on the news, and that generated questions and interviews, then all these exciting elements boiled down to excitable professors and artists contacting my mom about the ambition I behold and what a remarkable protégé I would be. It was all up to me, it was always up to me my mom would say, but I said yes just to see the bright lights remain in her eyes. Every bright shimmer that humanity ever shined would be perfectly captured in her eyes when it felt like things were falling into place, or when she was extremely happy about something.

My teenage weekends were spent in prestigious art studios and galas instead of parental-free house parties and crowded backseats. I learned a great deal from greatly dealt cards in the artistic community; plans of future gallery shows, painting series I could do, books I could write and illustrate, murals I must paint, taking commissions from people all over the world.

People lit up with something extraordinary when they saw my work. They loved to talk to me, it thrilled them to put a face to the miraculous work of art. And it all started with my mom. She's the one who started this, this whole thing.

Everyone saw something in me, except for myself. I thought it would be inevitable that someday I would find it, what this great gift's purpose is inside of me, what it is that I'm supposed to care so much about. But I haven't, and I've sunk into this perception that perhaps I won't. Hence the experimentation of excelled isolation.

3

Friend Match

I'm right on time; this is my first day helping someone. And I know I can do it. I'm equipped and ready, or at least I keep telling myself that through the deep breaths I take with every step. But as my eyes counted down to the 23rd apartment, I felt my confidence take a turn.

The door was collaged in what appeared to be scrap pieces of paper. Perhaps they were scribblings of stories, some bits were painted, and a few concert stubs were peering out; geez, just from the door, I feel like I'm approaching something I can't prepare myself for. Knocking my knuckles on it almost seems wrong because it feels like some intimate piece of art. Each piece radiates this personification as I'm trying to imagine their significance. And while my eyes are dancing from piece to piece, I softly apologize for the knock it's about to receive. I mentally remind myself of all the training I've completed and how hard I've worked to be where I am now. Damn near almost convinced myself too before the door opened.

With headphones draped around her neck, like a scarf that hasn't been tossed over the shoulder just yet, she looked puzzled, and with just the pass of a second, she now seemed weirded out. I felt how much I gripped the tangerine telegram in my hand out of nervousness. I lifted the message to read it while hoping it wasn't crinkled to the point of unprofessionalism.

This is the moment, my first L.A.F. Empath career-defining moment. Take a good breath, not too noticeable, and let's start out clear, confident, and positive.

In the mere seconds I had to collect myself, I took in her presence. Obviously, I can't efficiently know anything fully or deeply about her in only a few moments. Still, I can boldly state something about Rivers Talantirt in this instant: She is full heartedly a creative. If that wasn't apparent enough with the door, it read clearly with the immensely detailed scene she painted onto her entire right leg. I noticed this as I impulsively looked down before bringing the telegram up to read.

The raise of her eyebrow signaled my vocal cords to get moving, "Hello there, I have a C.C.R. for you-"Unexpectedly, I was interrupted.

"C.C.R., I don't see them with you, ya liar." She spoke in a playfully dull tone.

I could tell I was about to stammer my words, "I um, I'm sorry, what?" There it is.

"The band, Creedence Clearwater Revival. Forget it, sorry, you were saying."

Giving her a small half smile, I nodded. "Oh yes, right, good band. Um, this C.C.R. actually stands for Comfort Connection Request. I can read it to you now." I waited a moment to see if she had a witty rebuttal or wanted to hum a tune of Creedence Clearwater

Revival to test if I knew who she was talking about. But it appeared I was testing her patience, so I began reading.

"Rivs," I addressed with sincerity as I peeked for a glance at her eyes before returning to the delivery of words; she remained unimpressed.

"Please don't close your door this is important. I am worried about you. I don't want you to be alone, at least not for this day."

I glanced again at her eyes, which now had a stir of amusement and a decorated grin on her previously blank face to match it. She was leaning against the frame of her door with ease as I quietly cleared my throat to finish.

"Please do this for me; I know that will make you not want to do it but just, surprise me, okay? Love, Mom."

Looking up at the release of the last word, I saw that her demeanor changed yet again. She now displayed a combination of confused enlightenment, somehow.

This was my cue, "My name is Dutch; I work for the humanity service Lend a Friend," I felt compelled to hand her the tangerine card as proven evidence. After doing so, I quickly scanned my memories of training to remember if that was even allowed. Something about her presence made rules and sense warp and go out of focus. Or perhaps I'm just incredibly nervous, and I'm already screwing up. At least I can tell myself I was on time.

She observed the paper in what seemed like an obligation, and I began wondering if she would accept the service or not. I wasn't even sure what the protocol was if the service was rejected. But before my mind had time to spiral, thank God, she straightened out her back, let out a breath that allowed her to drop her shoulders, and welcomed me into her apartment. Without the accompaniment of words.

I tried to walk in as stoic as possible; this excitement started pulsing through me that I would have the opportunity to do the job I'd been training for. Humbly that racing feeling began to slow as I caught a whiff of a caramel candle that ignited some remanence that nearly stopped me in my tracks.

I'm not highly confident in many abilities but identifying candle scents is one of my personal badges of honor. For a brief season of my childhood, my father was the manager of a fancy candle store. *Heaven Scent*, quite the clever play on words. I shook my head just a tad to leave the candle nostalgia behind; it's time to get to work.

"I know I don't know your mother, but from reading her words, I can see that she cares deeply for you. Even if she's far away."

"Yea, Indie is deeply something for sure." She spoke without breaking her concentration on cleaning up the painting area she had made on the floor.

"Oh," I felt like we were starting to make a connection, "Is that your mother's name?"

"Sister's." Rivers blatantly replied as she gathered her used paintbrushes and placed them bristles first into a clean cup of water. It took only a moment for all the colors to bleed into each other. As I felt it was taking only a moment to confirm that I was indeed already failing at this job.

Maybe she misheard the message, or I wasn't speaking clearly enough. "Oh, actually, I said the message was from your mother, not your sister. I'm sorry, sometimes my diction is not the greatest." Hopefully, I can smooth this over, and we can get back on track.

Setting the cup of paintbrushes down, she now gave me her full attention, and boy was that a force to be reckoned with. Rivers scenic leg was propped out in front of her as the other stood straight, and her arms were crossed. "Are you a medium?" She asked in full-fledged confidence like I've never seen.

I haven't had the liberty of performing an impromptu spit-take, but that would have been the moment. I could feel the taken aback reaction flow through me and clearly translate to my body language, "I'm sorry, what? Um, no, no, I'm not."

Rivers looked me up and down in what appeared to be observation and annoyance. "The message is from my sister. This is her signature morbid attention-getting tactic that she uses on me." She uncrossed her arms and started to finish her sentence while she was in midmotion to return to cleaning up. "My mom died four years ago." Rivers held the cup in her hand and blew out the caramel candle.

Both the candle and my mind were blown. Rivers' sister wrote this message? Morbid seemed like an understatement, and my whole game plan just flew out the window.

"Look," Silencing my train of panicked thought. "I'm not familiar with the company you work for, but I'm not looking to get you in trouble with your boss or anything, so you can do your thing as long as I can do mine. Deal?" She stuck out her free hand marked with various colors, and we struck a deal as my hand met hers. "Good, well, I have some paint to wash off, so let's walk and talk, shall we?"

I nodded as she had already made her way to the kitchen to drop the paint brushes off and then walked to, I'm assuming, the bathroom. And now, as I walked through her apartment, I began to see even more of her personality.

Several walls were covered in paint. Thick, detailed layers of these beautiful landscapes. One large wall in Rivers' living room was painted as this meadow with gorgeous lively wildflowers. How in the world she achieved to make the painting give off a glow of warmth, I had no clue; it was so captivating.

The hallway wall to her bathroom was a deep dark blue oasis of stars and constellations. But they didn't seem like scientifically found constellations; these appeared to be ones she created. In small print beside them, she painted their names. I only caught a few: Stóri Bastarðurinn and Stórkostleg Tík. I wonder what language that is and what they mean.

She walked past them with hardly any attention; in all fairness, she's probably just so used to them. Then again, it seemed like she was walking past them with pride like she doesn't get to show these works off very often. In either case, I was dumbfounded, and even more so as we approached the bathroom. I cautiously stopped at the threshold, and she looked at me oddly.

"You can sit on the counter or the toilet with the seat down or something. Go ahead and give me your spiel, but park it and then keep your eyes closed and covered until I tell you to unmask yourself."

Quickly I picked my seat, which was her second gracious option.

And I accidentally smacked myself from covering my eyes so abruptly.

Because she was already getting undressed, and I did not want to see

anything. Rivers chuckled a little by the sound, and this was going

poorly. Wincing a little from the short-lived sting around my eyes, I

tapped into my L.A.F. Empath training.

"So, as I mentioned before, I work for the non-profit Lend a Friend. I'm

a trained Empath, which I know sounds ironic, but it's just the job title.

Anyway, so my job is to help you through today. People send in a request

for their loved ones to be accompanied on a particular day. After some

background checks and whatnot, that request is sent through the system

until a Friend Match is made. Which is what you and I are the

equivalents of, a Friend Match." I heard the water pour out and switch

to a controlled drizzle as the shower curtain drew back.

"I see. Essentially my sister posed as our dead mom, so you would come and be my friend for the entire day, which is our mom's death anniversary. That's your job?" The shower floor squeaked as she must have stepped inside, and the shower curtain closed. "You can unmask yourself. Thank you for your cooperation."

Following her blessing, my wimpy eyes adjusted themselves to the bathroom light. "Yes, I guess plainly said, that is sort of my job." I started to imagine how the colors were swirling and mixing at her feet and how cool that would be to see. I was disappointed in myself for not asking what she painted, but I didn't want her to think I was staring at her leg.

"I've kind of built my own motto for this job, and it's that with each Friend Match I have that's a new purpose I have the privilege of carrying. So today, this is my purpose, where all my attention and energy is."

"Well, that's sort of sweet," Her voice carried over the water, "How many of these purposes have you had?"

"This is my first, actually." I felt kind of nervous revealing that.

She let out an exaggerated awe and popped her head out of the shower. "I'm your first?" I was beginning to see Rivers' sense of humor, but that didn't yet rescue me from the knot in my throat.

"Oh, relax, please. I'm only joking." Returning to the shower with the curtain tightly closed, I heard a soap bottle open. "As your new friend, though, I feel I have the right to ask you some questions."

Okay, she really knows how to keep a person on their toes. "You have a point there, Rivers-"

"Rivs, I prefer Rivs, please."

"Rivs," I corrected, "I'm sure you don't really want to know anything about me. I'm really just here for you and to help you through today."

"How am I supposed to trust a friend I know nothing about? I'm not going to tell you anything deep and personal until I hear something remotely personal from you. I don't open up to people; that's not my thing, never has been, so you better dust off that empathy training of yours." Shooting straight from the hip, another personality trait was uncovered.

I was starting to feel even more uneasy; I wasn't expecting my Friend Match to ask me these questions even though she made some compelling points. And I began to feel like a hypocrite to my title and purpose as I so proudly claimed; I do not open up to people either. My own parents hardly know the closed-off sections of unprocessed shit I have scattered throughout me, and I am undeniably close to them. Maybe even too close. Like, *Lorelai* and *Rory Gilmore, Gilmore Girls* close. I just felt like if I said the things that hurt me inside, if I let them live in any place outside my mind, they would intensify and haunt me even more. Which I suppose is unhealthy, and the hypocrisy increases. Taking a deep breath, I decided a wall would come down in the sole pursuit of helping Rivs let hers down.

"Okay, can we promise to keep whatever is said in this bathroom a secret?" Without hesitation, her arm popped out of the shower as she lent her pinky. Sitting up and leaning over a little, my dry pinky momentarily latched onto her wet one as we sealed the promise and her water driblet arm returned.

"I'm also guilty of not opening up to people. Well, about certain things, I guess. That's why I applied for this job and have worked hard to learn and understand. I want to help others since I haven't been able to help myself. I don't know if that makes me selfish or stupid, but it's the truth I have right now." I paused to see if she wanted to chime in, but from our 'friendship' so far, I've learned that she is not shy about chiming in when she wants to.

"I have been struggling with, um, a body image and eating disorder for quite a few years now, and- "

"Wait, seriously? Are you being serious?" She bluntly questioned.

I let out a sigh to try and get the offense out of my tone, "Yea, it's a challenge I've been living with for a long time, and I've never told anyone." But I don't think it ultimately worked.

The shower turned off, and Rivs hand grabbed the floral printed towel hanging on the wall. She pulled it inside, and shortly after, she pushed the curtain aside and sat on the tub's edge wrapped in a long beach towel. Her legs were scene-free, and I apparently unlocked a new facial expression from her. She looked genuinely concerned.

"I am sincerely sorry for the way I reacted. That was extremely insensitive and not cool." Her voice sounded soft and comforting.

"Truthfully, I don't know much about eating disorders, especially from a male perspective, but that was really ignorant of me. I deeply apologize, and I am fully ready to be educated."

I could feel my eyes widen and then return to normal; wow, that was probably the sincerest and well-thought-out apology I've ever received. "I forgive you. It's okay. Body dysmorphia and eating disorders aren't really talked about from a male perspective; you're right." Clasping my hands together, I could feel them shake. Speaking these words out loud was overwhelming, and I think she caught on.

"Okay" Rivs also put her hands together but folded over the knee of her crossed leg. "A deal is a deal." Looking like she was conducting a very lax job interview; she also partook in the deep breath technique I used before opening up.
"My mom died four years ago by the greedy hands of ovarian cancer on this day." Rivs had subtle theatrics that I felt my parents would

appreciate. "That's why Indie sent that request, that and I haven't spoken to her consistently for a long time."

"I know it's been four years, but that can't be easy to deal with no matter how much time has passed." Geez, I felt like I was making it even harder. "I'm really sorry you went through that."
We sat in the silence of those words for a little while. For a minute there, I thought we were both waiting for her to air dry.

"What do you suggest we do?" Rivs frank voice was back on; she was a little challenging to navigate, and I presented the first option my scrambled mind could think of.

4

Baby Steps

"So, how long are we going to walk for?" I asked him, mildly irritated, mainly curious. I didn't want to be annoyed towards him; it was indirectly for my sister. Shooting the messenger, I know, I know.

"I don't know, until we feel better, I guess." I saw him shrug as he looked down at his feet and then back up to the sidewalk world in front of us.

It actually comforted me that he used the word 'we' like we were in this together. I didn't want to get too comfortable, though. I still don't know this guy. But it's almost a sweet deal that I could just unload my frustrations on this one-day friend and not have to deal with the aftermath of lingering talks on the matter.

"That seems fair enough," We walked on the sidewalk alongside the pretty leaves that fell. A friendly reminder from nature that even beautiful things fall at some point. "Should we just go back and forth and say stuff until we feel comfortable talking about the root of our problems?"

He glanced at me and smiled a little bit. "Geez, maybe you should have my job. You're better at this than I am."

"I wasn't trying to undermine you; you are doing a good job. I mean it when I say I don't open up to anyone. And I also don't really hang out with just anyone." I don't know why I felt obliged to reassure him, but lo and behold, here we are.

"I'm sorry I've been bitchy and probably hard to read, I'm seriously not used to talking to people, but that's a lame excuse. I've actually been in this loner practice lifestyle, like actively being lonely so I can focus on trying to focus on what my focus is supposed to be." I peeked from my peripheral to see if I cracked a smile.

Whatta score.

"One, you aren't bitchy. I can understand not being totally open

to a complete stranger arriving at your door and reciting a forged

message from your deceased mother. That's a free pass."

Well, well, score for him as well; that was funny.

"Two, that's a very interesting mission you've got on your hands.

Are you allowed to disclose any further details?"

I gave him a glance of approval for his rebuttal; not sure if he got

the gist but whatever. "It's an experiment I concocted myself. I wanted

to push the boundaries of loneliness, like truly lonely. I just felt like

there had to be another side to it. Like people didn't sit in loneliness

long enough to reach past the typical side effects and to this part where

they gain a new state of mind and emphasis."

"You're right; I don't know anyone who has allowed themselves

to sit in loneliness for that long. What's driven you to want to reach that? To get to the focus on the focus of your true focus as you so simply put."

Oh, he's good. I can tell he doesn't give himself enough credit. "That I'm going to have to unpack. And I'm not sure if I'm ready to yet." Just because he hitched a ride onto the wave of my humor doesn't mean I'm ready to wave pages of my diary in front of his face. "Let's revert to our original blueprint of back-and-forth banter."

Without proceeding with awkwardness, he agreed by continuing to talk. "I have two dads. I was adopted."

"That's pretty fascinating. Do you know your birth parents?"

"No, well, I know of the surrogate who carried me. She's a successful Intellectual Property Lawyer who was apparently irate during my delivery because I was 5 days late, and that's *not what they agreed upon*." Dutch's air quotes made me laugh.

"She sounds like a peach" We joined in on a laugh, and despite my experiment, it felt sort of nice to laugh *with* someone. "I didn't know my father either. My sister told me he dipped out for some mid-life crisis reason. You were a late bloomer, and as my mom would celebrate for my entire existence, I was on time. When's your birthday?"

"Summer baby, August 15th, yours?"

"Woah," I almost stopped walking for a second, "Mine's August 10th." But after my response, he stopped walking and looked at me as we froze.

"You said you were 5 days late?" Dutch nodded. "That's fricken weird."

"Just a lot," he said as we were both now bounded by weirdness.

"And you're 25, right?"

"Yep," Dutch answered, the puzzlement evident in his voice.

"Holy shit, no kidding, wow, this is wild." In continued bewilderment, we journeyed on. "So, are your dads cool?" Attempting to go back to our previous conversation before we jumped onto that mind-bender.

"They're pretty great, yea. Not gonna lie, though; my dads were hovering parents to an extent. I think they waited so long to have a child of their own that they didn't want me out of their sight once they did. Like they were pre-obsessed with me."

I chuckled a little at his wording, which he seemed okay with, so it must have been intentionally humorous. "Ah, the classic gay helicopter parents."

"Right, that total cliché," Dutch smirked and went to a slightly more serious tone. "I wouldn't have traded them for anything in the world, but man did I have some hell to pay throughout school."

I looked towards Dutch; he had his hands in his pockets and was watching his steps. "Wow, really? That sucks. People are the worst. Wait, before diving into that, what high school did you attend?"

"I went to Southeast."

"Ah, no educational relation, go on."

I got another small laugh from him. "Well put, and yes, people suck. Since I had two dads, that made people assume for some reason that I was also gay. Clearly, I am fully supportive of the LGBTQ+ community. Still, no one ever bothered to get to know me well enough to know that I don't identify as that."

"Might I ask, seeing as we've been friends for almost an hour now, what do you identify as?" I didn't know if I was crossing a line or not, but I wasn't going to see this guy again anyway.

"Demisexual, interested in women. Thanks for politely asking." Dutch gave me a crooked smile, which I took as a token of genuine gratitude. "To be completely honest, I was surrounded by a lot of toxic masculinity throughout middle school and high school. People assumed I was gay, so bullying and harassing me resulted in being immediately outcasted by many people. Thankfully I had a few friends, but I still received a lot of ridicule and physical, mental, and emotional pain."

Letting his words genuinely sink in so I could give him a meaningful response, I noticed that Dutch and I walked in sync for a few feet, which made me a little happy inside. "That's horrible. I can't believe you had to live through that. Bullies are the fricken worst."

I could feel him looking at me, "You were bullied?"

Giving him a nod, I half-reluctantly opened on the topic. "Yea, I was. Course, I probably made it a little easy for them. I wasn't shy about who I was. I walked around knowing that I was different. I think people weren't at that stage of life yet where they wanted to embrace what set them apart from others, so they stabbed me with their insecurities. I was probably a little *too* radical at times as well. In that setting, I may have rubbed people the wrong way. Not that I cared, and I still don't, to be honest. Suppose that's the product of being raised by a feminist flower child. I'm pretty thankful for that, though."

I took a moment to breathe, I felt like I was talking super fast, and it felt out of character. To which I decided to counteract it with some factual humor.

"I got the delicate nickname of Rivvie Commie because I liked to correct the white-washed history spewed out in class." Looking from the corner of my eye, I saw the corner of his mouth curl up. And I think he wasn't remorseful for opening up to me, and I think I was beginning to feel the same way.

We walked silently for a little while, which I'm glad for. If I'm going to feel comfortable enough to open up to this guy, like really tell him my shit, I need to feel at ease when we're saying nothing at all.

Maybe that's putting too much pressure on the guy. He's just trying to do his job. But a part of his job is occupying me on this day, and if he doesn't have to talk for part of it, maybe I'm making it easier on him. Let's be honest; this is probably not what he expected for a first client.

Ultimately, I decided that if I was the one who created the silence, I should be the one to break it after it felt like a satisfactory amount of time.

"If anyone ever asked me my favorite animal when I was younger, I would tell them it was a Sphinx to weird them out." Man, I really thrived off that. I suppose, in some way, I still do if I'm telling him this tidbit.

The softest chuckle came out of him; honestly, I was relieved. "Well, you got me there; you are certainly one of a kind Rivs." He glanced at me but then changed his reaction, "Wait, hold on here, are we talking like Greek Mythology Sphinx or Egyptian Sphinx? This can be very telling of a person."

Dutch was actually pretty damn funny with a nice swirl of clever, just my speed. "Oh, you know, any Sphinx is a good Sphinx to me." He damn well almost beat me at my own weird game. We would have laughed just now if we had been friends, like true friends. But instead, it was like we checked another box of comfortability in our minds. If our odd relationship had the cards to bloom after 24 hours, we would have the natural opportunity to laugh in the future. But I don't think that will happen.

"I'm sorry if I've been making this difficult," I blurted out, maybe so fast, so I didn't have time to change my words. "My sister's note threw me off, the day is ridiculously sucky, and I'd be dumb if I tried to convince myself that I haven't been lost for a while."

"You're not dumb, I don't know a whole lot about you even with the interesting fact you generously gave me, but I know you're definitely not dumb." He paused for a few moments; our feet must have been on autopilot while our minds, or at least mine, were racing. Dutch cleared his throat softly, "Maybe we were supposed to help each other not feel so lost anymore. I've been hired to help you through today, but without sounding too overzealous, I think we were meant to help each other with more than that. Like we've been carrying the other's compass for quite some time, and today is the day we exchange them and then carry on with the rest of what our lives are supposed to be? Like newfound confidence and clarity?"

"That was a bit overzealous." We looked at each other simultaneously, "But I like it, and I'm willing to bet on it." He gave me a smile like it was the first time someone allowed his mind to speak out his true authentic thoughts, and it wasn't obliterated.

"I mean the thing with our birthdays; that's just too weird to *not* mean something."

We lingered in eye contact for a few seconds before I saw him relax his arms with his hands in his pockets, and we both looked forward. "That's what I'm saying," Dutch responded excitedly but calmly.

The two of us kept on walking. Together. And there was something therapeutic about our pace, both in our steps and conversation. I could feel layers of myself unfolding. Now wanting to be seen, I could feel the awkward stranger tension dissolve slowly between us. And what I saw up ahead would be the perfect setting for comfortable vulnerability.

"Hey, wanna sit in a vinyl booth and eat the best fries you've ever had on this side of the city?" With a quick observation to see if the idea landed or not, Dutch made me mirror his smirk; it was so contagious.

5

Best Fries & No Lies

We walked into a quirky place called Gilligan's Slice. Upon walking into the aged establishment, I gathered where the inspiration came from. The walls were covered entirely in the old sitcom *Gilligan's Island* memorabilia.

Posters, signed items, hats, coconuts, it even looked like a few cast members came in here once and took a picture with the owner. There were tacky island decorations in places where the walls weren't covered with souvenirs.

The diner wasn't that large; there were two sides for dining and a lunch counter. There was a T.V. mounted in the corner on both dining sides and set in black and white with reruns of *Gilligan's Island*. As for the folks at the lunch counter, it sounded like a baseball game was broadcasting.

Following Rivs, she made her way to the left side and sat in the 3rd booth against the wall. All in all, I could see the appeal of this place. It was pretty unique, much like the person sitting across from me.

"What a riot this place is. I'm actually surprised I've never heard of it."

"Well, if your theory is right, maybe you weren't supposed to come across this place until *I* showed it to you."

She gave me a cunning grin and then caught the waiter's attention. He was dressed in a red shirt and a white bucket hat and taking a look at the décor around me, I placed that he was dressed as a character from the show.

"Hi there, we'll take a basket of fries and" She broke her concentration off the waiter and gave it to me. "Do you like coffee?"

A bit unprepared, I nodded as she turned back to the waiter.

"And two coffees, please. If you have French vanilla creamer, that would be deluxe." She gave the waiter a smile, and he flashed one back to us before taking care of another table.

As I was taking in the atmosphere, I scooted a little further into the booth while Rivs stretched her legs out, and her feet rested on my side. At least she was getting comfortable; maybe we could get somewhere.

"Thank you for bringing me here and showing me this place. I look forward to trying these fries you speak highly of."

Her arms crossed and slouching a little, she gave me a half smile. "Yea, no problem. I think you'll like them; they're addicting." Rivs kind of seemed distracted now.

The hoppy waiter returned with our coffees, housed in collector cups with the *Gilligan's Island* cast member's faces on them. He set down a small bowl with the requested French vanilla creamers.

"How do you take your coffee?" I asked her while I was pulling out my own coffee specifications.

"I don't drink coffee." Rivs flatly answered while her eyes glanced around the room.

"Oh," I responded, trying not to sound too confused as I poured in my desired single creamer and sugar packet. While stirring the contents, I too looked about the diner; I accidentally made eye contact with an old man. We gave one another a short nod. I saw customers watching the black-and-white show and laughing in nostalgia. Then I looked back at Rivs and noticed she moved the cup of coffee to her side like we had another companion just in the restroom.

"So, you've been here before?"

Now her full attention returned to me. Although I haven't experienced much of it, I know it's powerful and shouldn't be taken for granted. With her arms crossed still, but more for a comfortable position, not in frustration, she nodded in confirmation.

"Yep, I'm kind of surprised I'm here now, to be honest."

Then again, she broke from my eyes to look about the diner, not with her whole body but just the gaze in her eyes. Eventually, they circled back to me but not before she looked down and breathed in for a moment. When she looked at me, the look in her eyes was completely different from before. Like she had come to terms with something. Like she was letting go.

"I guess this is the part where I let you in," Rivs said in a cinematic way. Which I could tell was purposeful from the short-lived smirk she gave me that switched back to the melancholy of the situation.

"Indie sent this request or whatever it's called-"

"C.C.R."

Rivs glared, "Yea, that. Look, on a side note, I think that should be reconsidered. I was truly disappointed to not see the renowned *Creedence Clearwater Revival* at my backdoor." Once again, the tiniest smirk came off her. I could see that sarcasm, comedic relief, and cinema-inspired moments were her coping skills.

"I see what you did there, and I'll see what I can do." Giving her the best *quirky male friend from an indie movie* response I could muster.

"Very well, moving on. Before my mom got *super* shitty sick, this was our place. That apartment I live in was our apartment; we'd walk here and chill out, bring a board game, eat fries, talk for a hella long time."

"And drink coffee?" I asked, hoping to make a connection.

"Mom would. I don't consume any substances that could alter my state of mind. Well, most things, maybe there are some foods and sugars that have that ability, but I don't know. I've never smoked, experienced drugs, drank alcohol, or had sex. I've just always wanted my mind to remain clear because I like the oasis I've built within it."

I knew I was looking at her in astonishment. I couldn't help it; it was utterly admirable and fascinating to me. What a dedicated creative, my goodness.

"Anyway," She broke my gaze, as I was hoping it wasn't too weird. "Mom told me at a young age that coffee is addicting. She would get headaches if she didn't drink it. So that was the first thing I banned myself from. But I ordered it here because it just didn't feel right not having a cup of coffee on the table while I was here. And then I didn't want you to think I was weird, so I asked if you wanted some."

"Sincerely, I don't think you're weird." Rivs almost seemed like she was leaning into what I was saying as if it were words she rarely heard. "I admire what you told me about keeping your mind clear. That's really hard for me to do. And thank you for opening up to me about those special moments between you and your mom. I can totally see why you guys loved it here."

With an approving nod, she slightly smiled while looking around again, "We really did love it here. We were regulars for a while." Rivs eyes looked down again as she pulled her legs back to her side of the booth, brought them up to her chest, and laid her arms on the table with her hands folded.

Rivs looked at me, and I could see she was ready to talk more. "I haven't seriously talked to Indie in, I don't even know how long. Probably since mom's funeral. She's tried to send me emails and texts, but they're usually riddled with guilt, and I'm not buying that. This C.C.R. is probably the most sisterly thing she's done, and it's covered in shit by her using mom to get my attention." She scoffed, but it was intertwined with the lightest amusement. "Then again, it's pretty genius of her."

I was listening, truly and genuinely listening, and it felt so rewarding to have built up this trust between us that she felt like she could talk to me. And I was sincerely enjoying her company in the odd yet comforting atmosphere of Gilligan's Slice.

"Indie is four years older than me. After graduating, she and her high school boyfriend moved to Oregon, and they've been there ever since. Mom and I flew to Oregon for their wedding and when her first child was born. Ethan. But Indie just kind of had her own life going on over there that rarely included us, so it became just mom and me. I was already a loner, so mom became like my best friend in a way. We moved into that apartment because it was more affordable. Mom was diagnosed with ovarian cancer right after I graduated high school. It felt like it happened back-to-back." She took a pause to gather some thoughts and take another breath. Perhaps this was another coping skill of hers.

"I was supposed to have an apprenticeship with a fantastic artist, Sofia Bianchi, who wanted to take me under her wing in the big windy city. My living arrangements were even made with this cool woman Georgia Sohn who runs like a misfit's boarding house. And from there, tons of doors would open. Or so Sofia told me. But I canceled it because someone needed to be with mom."

Once again, my eyes widened. She was a fantastic storyteller, but then the reality of her words sank in, and I felt all these wonders of her opportunity slip away. I couldn't help but feel sad.

"I never ever resented mom for that, not even in the dark moments. Those days I had with her are precious, and I can't even imagine the ending of her life being any other way than how it played out. But it made me angry that Indie didn't even try to help me. I was drowning in this newfound responsibility while mourning the loss of that remarkable opportunity. Still, she couldn't even attempt to help me find another solution for mom."

Rivs focused on her hands for a moment; mine was still wrapped around the warmth of the novelty *Gilligan's Island* mug. The ambiance of the diner occupied the air between us for a minute until she cleared her throat and looked back up.

"Hearing myself finally say those heavy thoughts out loud kind of felt like ridiculous, in all honesty," She raised one hand as her palm now supported her head. At the same time, she leaned in more toward our conversation, like she was amid realization.

"Maybe I pushed her away, I don't know. But my problem now is that I have lost my drive for artistic purposes since I passed up on working with Sofia Bianchi and the day that mom died. And for lack of better words and at the expense of sounding dramatic, my art and imagination are everything I have and am. My mom was the one who fueled it for me. She always reminded me that I had a duty to this world and myself to create art and to tell the stories that lived inside my funny head. I never learned how to carry that out myself. I've been searching for my artistic purpose again, and I'm afraid I'll never find it. And then I'm even more afraid I've never had it, and it was purely just my mom filling my head with wonders. That really doesn't sound like her, though."

With a natural pause for me to jump into the conversation, I daringly took my chance. "If I may, I knew you were artistically gifted just by walking up to your apartment door." I chuckled a little bit, "In fact, I was afraid to even knock on it because it just looked so cool, and it felt disrespectful to do something as mediocre as knocking on a work of art."

"Ah, you see, that's the beauty of the messy door, as my mom so lovingly called it. It brings character to the ordinary. Or makes us a bigger target for random burglaries."

Rivs smiled for a millisecond, relieved to have had a little comedy after such a long string of serious sentences, I'm assuming. "Dutch?"

I felt myself perk up at the sound of her addressing me. I nonchalantly tried to redeem my over-telling body language.

"Yea, Rivs?"

She flagged down our preppy waiter, "Wanna play a game with me?"

6

Your Turn

I knew it had been a while since I had been here, but the old place really couldn't have changed that much. This establishment pulses off routine and nostalgia.

"Hi again, could we order a game, please?" Taking a quick glance at Dutch, I wanted to catch his reaction. I'll be honest, I like being noticed for my clever moments.

The waiter reached into his waisted apron and pulled out a separate little laminate menu that listed the current board games in stock. That I knew were held behind the lunch bar counter. Taking the menu and placing it between Dutch and me, I asked him what sounded good.

"My goodness, hmmm," He pondered for a moment. "I'm almost certain it would be a crime if we parted ways and didn't play *Candy Land* at least once."

This was the first time he caught me off guard and brought out a giddy smile from me. I felt my face scrunch up in a grin as I relaxed my facial muscles and requested our game from the waiter. As he returned with the well-used *Candy Land*, he also refreshed our drinks and brought our order of fries.

"We should leave him a big tip. That drop-off and service were phenomenal. Did you see how he balanced the board game, fries, and fresh pot of coffee? All with a *Gilligan-approved* smile." Dutch chirped and marveled at the fries before looking at me.

"It's cool to see the humorous part of your personality. You're funny." I admitted before reaching my hand toward the basket of fries. "Dig in; you gotta let me know what you think of these babies." After eating a few fries, I set up our sure-to-be intensely candied, rectangular, colorful journey.

"Holy shit," Dutch uttered as my head shot up in his direction just as I placed one of the characters on their plastic peg. "Pardon my

French, but goodness gracious, you weren't kidding. These are the best fries ever."

"Don't pull my leg now, Dutch; we have a good thing going here." Poking a little fun now that I have some bearing on his sense of humor.

"Oh no, these fries can only evoke truth. They're so holy." He ate 2 more after his bold statement, "Yea, these are officially the best."

We laughed briefly, and then he gave me a gentle smile.

"Thanks for showing me, for bringing me here. My stomach is also very grateful."

I gave him a nod. I didn't feel like mending some kind of sentimental moment at the moment; *Candy Land* needed to be set up.

After doing so, we picked our pieces and played a quick best 2 out of 3 Rock-Paper-Scissors to see who would start. And so, the fates have decided, I was to grace the cardboard haven first.

"Congratulations on your path of victory as I foresee you winning this game." Dutch applauded me as I laughed and reminded him of this game's *mighty* skill of merely picking up a card and moving your piece to the correct color square. "Should we make the game a little more interesting?"

"You mean, more interesting than a fictional sugar foundation kingdom? By all means, please, my curiosity is hooked."

"You're gracious." He authoritatively sealed our now established sarcastic yet genuinely intentional banter. "Shall we be granted to ask one another a question at the end of each turn?"

Giving him a less than serious eye roll, I released a breath before answering. "I suppose it would be in our best interest, this being your job and all."

Dutch shrugged neutrally; perhaps he didn't know how to answer, so I spared us the awkward pain and answered him.

"Proposition accepted."

My turn was as thrilling as the first turn in *Candy Land* can be, and I thought of a question quickly, one to ease us into this now profoundly personal game.

"What's a memory you have with your parents that you treasure? Since I brought you here, somewhere special to my mom and me, you could take me somewhere special to you. Via your descriptive storytelling."

He smiled a bit while thinking. "Although I'm sorry to say I won't be as nearly a good storyteller as you, I'll do my best. That is a good question."

As the thinking continued, I grew a little excited to hear his answer, to get more depth of who he is. Who is this politely slightly mysterious Dutch?

"My dads and I would go biking a lot; that was a big thing of ours. We'd ride on nearby trails, but our biggest annual biking tradition was traveling with the bikes on the back of the car up to my grandma's in Maine. Biking there felt like you were being filmed for the next coming-of-age film, and you were lucky enough to be the star." His eyes were caught up in memory for a moment as he met my smiling but observing eyes to finish the story.

"Sorry, got kind of carried away. But that's probably one of my best memories with my parents, biking in Maine. Reflecting back now as an adult, I really appreciate that my parents made it a point to create a lot of memories with me out in nature." Dutch adjusted how he was sitting, almost as though he was simultaneously getting more comfortable in his seating position and speaking to me.

"It's like, you kind of grow out of some of the toys you were bought as a kid, or even the games you'd play, or the jungle gyms you could slide through, but growing up with nature, you find that you don't outgrow it, it grows with you. I didn't really get that until now, weirdly enough."

I could feel myself smiling and smiling differently. I officially got to step inside this person's mind, a person I have hardly known. What an honor to cross the vulnerable threshold.

Before Dutch picked up a card, he glanced at me. "That may have been over-answering your question," he smirked a little before moving his piece to an orange-colored rectangle and then thinking of a question. "Since I kind of had a revelation of being thankful to have grown up with nature. What's something you're grateful to have had in your childhood that you now see in your adulthood?"

"Well, damn Dutch, that's a good question." I unapologetically proclaimed just as he took a sip of his coffee and laughed a little while drinking it. Thankfully, I wasn't in the caffeinated splash zone.

I chuckled with him, though, "Oh geez, sorry about that. Okay, let's see." I pretended to stroke a beard, an imaginary beard, but if the universe had thrown me in as a fella by golly, I would have rocked the most luscious beard.

"My mom's feminism and growing up in that atmosphere. She was a badass feminist." I decided to also get comfortable. Perhaps I was mirroring him a little bit.

"She founded this group called Stanton Lasses, Stanton as in Elizabeth Cady Stanton. She was one of the first feminists to like organize a group and be a public advocate in the U.S., at least as far as I know. I should do some more research. Anyway, my mom and these strong, awesome women would meet at our house about twice a month. They would put together scholarships for local women, volunteer to help women in need, and provide education on women's rights and history. I don't know they were just so awesome I can't describe it."

I looked around at the restaurant's occupants while telling the story and occasionally at my hands. But when I dared my eyes to look at my singular audience, he seemed to be in awe and fascination. Like he was actually listening to me. How exhilarating.

"I remember an Elizabeth Cady Stanton quote was painted on our kitchen wall. Mom had the idea during one of their meetings. And a group member had a skill for the brush and grabbed ready-to-go utensils from her car and got to work. That's how those badasses operated; they were ready to go. Every morning before school, I would stand in the kitchen, with my backpack on and waiting for Indie and my mom to get ready, so we could head out, and I would read that quote. I can't even fathom how many times I must have read it."

Dutch chimed in, "Wow, that's so profound. I have a feeling you may remember it now; may I be so bold?"

Like a singer being asked to serenade, I bashfully shuffled through the memory box in my mind and gathered the quote for him. *"The moment we begin to fear the opinions of others and hesitate to tell the truth that is in us, and from motives of policy are silent when we should speak, the divine floods of light and life no longer flow into our souls."*

"Holy moly, that is the most amazingly worded and truth-dripping statement I've ever heard. Like, dead serious."

He reached for some more fries and ate a few while also digesting the words of the powerful Elizabeth Cady Stanton. "You know, I think you've embedded those words into your life more than you may realize."

Whelp, he caught me; I was intrigued. "Is that so? Please, enlighten me." I politely requested and indulged in some fries.

Dutch began to speak his theory into our *Candy Land* experience existence with his *Gilligan's Island* novelty mug in his hand. As if he was giving a rare lecture on a world-shaking thesis.
"From what I know of you so far, it seems like you've done a pretty good job of not caring whatsoever of other's opinions because you do you without hesitation. And you do this to stay authentic to yourself, of course. But also to live within the creativity that you've created. The divine floods of light and life flow through you indeed. As I mentioned before, I saw that even from your apartment door."

"Hmm, you rhyme now, huh?" I gave him some sass while he took a swig of his coffee and waved me off. "No, but in all seriousness, that is a grand analysis you have on me. You're sure this is your first, whatever this is called?"

"A C.C.R., yes, it is. I've talked to quite a few people on the helpline, but honestly, the conversations we've been having have been nothing like I've ever experienced."

We looked at one another like we were instituting a new milestone in our brief relationship.

"I enjoy talking with you." Before I could say anything, he gave me a quick smile and spoke again. "I believe it's your turn."

Nodding in agreement, we sealed that part of our conversation and forged on to the next.

Moving my piece to a purple space, I needed a lighthearted question. After that, Dr. Phil meets *Hallmark* shit. "What's a weird moment you can recall happening to you?"

Dutch didn't look super prepared for this question as he was for the others, or so it seemed. "Although I know I give off a powerful aura of fascination, I'm sorry to reveal that I am actually not very interesting. I don't think anything too weird has happened to me before."

"Nope, I don't believe that for a fricken second," Crossing my arms and raising my eyebrow at him. "Go ahead, think about if, for a moment, your life is far more interesting than you give it credit for."

A tad bit reluctant, he paused the gears that, from what I could see, were constantly moving in his head, and he solely thought about my question. I felt honored to have that much intentional energy and genuine thought to a question I produced. And check that out; something clicked.

"Alright, alright, alright."

"Ah ha, turns out your life is interesting after all, huh, Matthew McConaughey?"

He blushed for a split second at the connection of my lame and overplayed joke, "Okay, yes, yes, I did think of something. Kind of small, but I suppose it fits the criteria of your question."

Nodding in anticipation as I snagged a couple of fries, he dramatically pretended to clear his throat. However, from the little crinkle between his eyes, it seems that maybe he *did* clear his throat.

"My dad would take me to different parks when I was younger; that was one of our special bonding things. We'd go to nearby towns and check out their parks, and sometimes there were some pretty neat ones. One time, this one had a castle theme, and that was like a fever dream; it was so cool. But anyway, this memory takes place at a pretty ordinary park. I don't remember much about it or even where it was. But sparked out of nowhere, I made a friend on the playground. Her name was Danny, and it was like an unspoken link that we had become friends. We just started playing together like we had always been friends and were simply meeting up at the park like we always do. She was particularly talented at monkey bars; I swear she could skip 5 bars at a time."

I knew my eyes were closed while he was replaying his memory, I wanted to see it for myself in my mind, and when I opened my eyes, a question slipped out. "That's literally the most wholesome thing, why did you declare that a weird thing that's happened to you?"

Dutch nodded as if accepting that it wasn't typical weird, but it's how he categorized it in his memory department.

"I guess it's weird because that is the only friend I can recall where I wasn't misinterpreted. I was just accepted right off the bat as a friend." Dutch swallowed his words and produced further ones to explain. "When people saw my dads, they would, for some bizarre reason, label me as gay too, as I've mentioned. And with that, I was never good enough as a *'guy'* or *'dude'*. Because I was apparently untraditional '*masculinity*'. So being friends with Danny, even if it was just one afternoon when I was 10 years old, gave me an example of what a good friend would look like. Maybe even a small sliver of truly finding it."

"Well, damn it, Dutch, you're gonna make me cry and tear stain this *Candy Land* board."

A tad bit unexpectedly, he laughed, "Truly, it's okay. I've been learning more and more about myself and what I went through in my childhood and adolescence, and I know things will get better."

Dutch smiled at me, "They already have." He really was nice to talk to. "Alright, before I ask a question, I would love to hear if you have a weird occurrence that also happened to you. You must have quite the pile to sift through."

Putting my hands up in surrender, I began to sift, as he put it, through my memories to find one I was willing to share. He took the opportunity to grub on a few more of the best fries ever.

"Okay, not too long ago, I was in the waiting room for a simple routine dentist appointment, and I brought my sketch pad with me to pass the time. I was doing my own thing when I felt like someone was like watching me, so I peered up a little, and sure enough, across the room, this lady with an outfit that I can only describe as *Mr. Noodle* meets Broadway, "

"Wait, I am so sorry for interrupting this riveting story, but just to get a reference check, you are indeed referring to *Mr. Noodle* as in the mime-ish clumsy fella from *Elmo's World*, correct?"

"Correct."

"Excellent; please proceed."

The conversation between us was becoming effortless, which I was almost going to question, but I internally decided to feed off it instead.

"So the eye contact between us is made, accidentally, for a mere 2 seconds, and that is apparently her signed permission slip to come over to me. She hastily takes a seat, and I close up my sketchbook, wondering what in the world she's going to say, and then she asks me if I have recently lost my mother."

Dutch's amusement shifted to speculation and anxiousness, similar to my feelings when this all happened.

"I gave her a face, pretty much the face you're making now, and I said something like, '*Yepp, little over 2 and a half years ago.*' And she gasps. The waiting room population, or the audience at this point, is pretending not to be engaged in this conversation, but they totally are. Hell, even the receptionists were, as I could see from the corner of my eye. The Broadway rummaging closet lady proceeds to tell me that she is a medium and my mother is here and that my mother wants me to know that she is at peace and that I should be too. She paused for a moment, almost like she was listening to someone talk, and then she placed her hand on mine and said, '*Your mother told me that she wants you to get back to your gifts*'. I didn't know what to say, so I thanked her, and then by the grace of the universe, my name was called."

Dutch's eyes were wide and wild with curiosity. He had just finished eating a handful of fries like he was at the movies. "Holy shit, that's insane!"

Laughing in agreement, I took some fries myself, "It was insane and random, I don't really know if I believe what happened, but oh well, it happened. Your turn."

"Fair enough," Folding his hands in thought and then separating them once he became inspired. "What is a guilty pleasure of yours? Could be anything, really."

I think he picked up that I felt hesitant to answer.

"By all means, I can think of a different question, there's no pressure at all, but if it makes you feel better, I'll share one of mine if you share yours."

I felt like a child that was just offered candy, and my hypothetically small sticky hand lunged for that fast. "Deal. My guilty pleasure is red Kool-Aid."

"Oh, please, be serious." He always had an air of proper to him. It was funny to me.

"Oh, but I am. As I disclosed before, I do not engage with substances, but my guilty poison is red Kool-Aid, which has been since I was a child. There's just something about that splash of red that gets me giddy." Shrugging and simultaneously feeling like I shrugged off the smallest meaningless amount of weight, I mischievously grinned as I tossed a fry at him. "Reap what you sow."

Dutch took the fry and, without pause, ate it and then playfully deeply sighed as his eyes wandered about Gilligan's Slice in thought. "As you wish." His eyes came back to me with their verdict.

"I have watched the movie *Pride and Prejudice*, the 2005 adaptation, so many times I couldn't even give you a ballpark number. My dads showed it to me when I was like 13 years old, and it's been a staple in my life ever since."

I returned to the Rolodex of movies I'd seen and recalled it. "Oh, yea, with Keira Knightley, right?"

A dorky expression captured him whole. I think he transported into an entirely new person now, "Yes, yes, that's the one. Oh my gosh, someone else who witnessed greatness, what a breath of fresh cinematic masterpiece air."

He performed an exaggerated chef's kiss, which I was totally enjoying.

Still, as he met my gaze, I saw in his eyes the transition back to the Dutch

I had been conversing with before.

Which didn't bum me out completely, I liked the company of

both, but I wondered what made this other side of him retreat. Well, I

mean, besides the fact that he was technically working. I kind of keep

forgetting that bit.

"Alright, Miss Red Kool-Aid, you're up." For a split second, he

sounded like a first-day-on-the-job tee-ball coach.

Making all the proper *Candy Land* checks and balances, I was trying to

think of a question that may make him open up a little more. Especially

after the dinner show he just put on. He's already shared quite a lot of

info with someone who has been about 75% cooperative, but my

curiosity is more potent than my courtesy at the moment.

"What's one thing you like about yourself and one thing you wish you could cut off from your identity?"

He wasn't exactly stunned by this question, but he didn't look thrilled to answer it; I can't say I would be either, but here we are.

"I guess I like that I'm a pretty punctual person. Course, it also drives me crazy sometimes. I'll internally applaud myself when I make it on time to where I have to be because my brain likes to schedule everything down to the minute when I'm by myself. So in my downfall, I get really hard on myself if I'm even a minute off. I just feel super thrown off."

Taking a pause, he grinned. "That didn't really sound like something I liked about myself, huh?" It was an ironic grin, seemingly.

"Anyway, something I wish I could cut off from my identity," Dutch pondered for a few moments, looking at the kingdom of the sugar that lay before us.

"Not to get like dark, I guess that's sort of implied in the question, but I'd want to take my body dysmorphia away. I want to have a healthy relationship with food and with myself. It's a really exhausting cycle, and I'm honestly genuinely surprised that I'm even eating these fries with you now. And that you made me feel comfortable enough to do that; it may seem mundane and ordinary, but that was huge for me, actually. I had to try really hard to do that."

I felt a sense of honor that he said that to me, and I've felt way more comfortable with him than I have with anyone else in quite some time. Clearing my throat quietly, maybe to buy even just a second to gather the right words to say, our eyes met up to continue the conversation.

"I don't know if I have the place to say this, being that we've just met today and all, and I don't have any prior knowledge of your journey with this awful disorder. But from my limited perspective, I think you should be proud that you could eat those fries without a second thought. Because you truly deserve to have that peace of mind, to have those beginning steps to your healing process from having lived with that disorder for so long. Dude, I honestly can't even imagine."

Dutch looked taken back, but only for a split second. The next emotion to come rushing down his face was calmness, accompanied by a sigh of relief. I think some of his tension went away.
"That felt relieving just to speak out loud to a person who's like my age and is cool at the expense of sounding dorky. A peer, in other words." Dutch's eyes wandered over the fries. They looked to be overthinking for a moment; perhaps he'll eat some again later.
"Would you like to answer that question?"

Giving him a cringy face, I laughed and tried to focus on my inner self, which isn't that hard given the solitude experiment I've been living in.

"I guess something I like is my imagination. I'm able to escape through it pretty much every day. According to my sister, some could argue that's my downfall too."

"She's straight up told you that?"

"Maybe not those words exactly, but with that point, yes. Indie would say things like, 'You're *so anti-social. Stop being so weird around people*' and '*You need to get out of your head and enter the rest of the world with us.*' Typical charming older sibling knowledge like that."

"You know, sometimes I'd wonder what it would have been like if I had an older sibling or just a sibling in general, but with that insiders look, I think I'm past it."

A nice dash of comedic relief; he understands the drift alright. Pretending to bow for my services, I continued, "I am grateful for my imagination and creativity. But when I seriously ask myself the other side of the question and listen for the echoing answer throughout myself and hear it ricochet up my bones and out my mouth, it kind of freaks

me out."

Dutch's head turned a little in curiosity and concern. I didn't

even know what my face looked like right now.

"Son of a bitch, maybe Indie was right to have contacted you

guys and your C.C.R. whateverness."

Exhaling, I looked at Dutch, and I could tell that my voice would sound

slightly different when I spoke.

"I don't have any motivation; I can't see a purpose even though,

ironically, I can see I have a wild gift for art. But I may have lost

something worse; I haven't seen much *good* humanity since my mom

died."

7

Let's Walk

I thought about saying something quirky and silly like *'I think the sidewalk missed our soles,'* but that sounded stupid before it even left my mouth.

After a bit longer, I spoke up once I noticed we were walking in similar strides, one leg after the other.

"I stand by my prediction I made at the beginning of the game; I think you would have won if we had finished. You were pretty far ahead of me." Glancing over to see her reaction, I looked just in time to see her hands up in surrender to my board game forecasts.

"I will say I did have a pretty good lead going on. I was skipping over sun-dyed colored rectangles left and right." Along with her enticing descriptions, as I should suspect by now from such a creative like her, she also chopped at the air in front of her with her last few words. Her silliness made me laugh, and it made me forget that I was technically on the clock.

"So, Dutch, can I ask you something?" Rivs spoke in a different tone, almost like a verbal signal that we were changing subjects. Apparently a more serious one.

"But of course, ask away." My hands retreated to my pockets, as they usually do when someone asks me a question. Perhaps because I wish, in a way, I could just shove myself in a pocket full of blankets and solitude when I'm asked a question.

"It's two, actually. May I continue?"

With a smile and nod, I granted the proceeding. My hands remained in their lint hideaway.

"This is your first time doing this aspect of your job, the C.C.R.; how do you think it's going? How're you doing?"

I was thankful to have already been looking at the sidewalk and my feet as we walked while she asked me this question because I felt my eyebrows look at each other and then raise in suspicion. What kind of angle does she have in asking me that? She could just be exercising some amount of compassion, sure, but that didn't seem to fit her puzzle for some reason.

Alas, I have nothing to hide in answering truthfully.

"I think it's going well; my job is to be there with you through this day and to process whatever you may need to. I'm feeling alright. I wasn't really expecting to tell you vulnerable things about myself that wasn't really covered in our training, so maybe I shouldn't have done that. But to be honest, it felt right and natural to do so. I can't expect you to open up to me if I'm unwilling to do the same."

Now I focused on her, and she seemed pleased with my answer. To whatever extent her goal was in asking me.

"I'm glad, and thank you." Rivs liked to be purposefully unclear at times, so I've learned. Or I may not understand her rhythm of conversational language.

"Moving onto our next question on the docket, which is an amusing word to say, do you like baking, or have you tried it?"

This time she saw the humor and puzzlement on my face, and she almost dared to mirror it, but her facial muscles stood their ground in a stern curiosity.

"I must admit, I wasn't expecting that question, but then again, that is your shtick. I do baking on occasion, yes, just simple things, though. Or shall I say, *dough*."

Rivs glared at me, but her smile was totally onboard with the pun. "I'll give you that one Dutch, only because I like your style, and that was rather clever."

Her demeanor shifted back to her previous state of mind before the impromptu pun. "Have you made a big batch of cookies before?"

Reverting to my baking memories, I did recall a few late-night baking sessions with my dad. And another for a bake sale to raise money for new school library furniture.

"Yes, I believe I have. If your next question is what kind, I will do the liberty of saying chocolate and butterscotch chip."

With a gentle hit on the arm from her, which I quickly realized was a friendly touch, she nodded. "Nice, nice, that sounds delicious. Butterscotch, I gotta remember that."

"It's a game changer, just saying."

"My life feels altered, and I ain't mad about it."

"As you shouldn't, butterscotch is madly underrated."

"Dutch, you're a gem," She laughed and then stopped in her tracks, looking past me. "Woah, now *I'm* about to alter yours. Check it out,"

Turning around, I saw what she was pointing to, and a smirk covered my face. "Hmm, looks like the universe is handing us a drink." Pivoting back to Rivs, she was already crossing the street and waving her arm for me to follow.

It felt inspiring to follow her. Even if it was just merely walking up to a child's Kool-Aid stand. It felt like we were about to step onto a train in a country we had never been to, to see sights we'd only swiped through on Pinterest. With the hours we've spent together and the ones we have remaining, every time I feel like I've got a grip on who she may be, she throws me another costume change.

As we approached the young entrepreneur's stand, Rivs pulled out a wallet and then looked them in the eye. A bit intensely, actually. Hopefully, in a humorous way.

"What kind of Kool-Aid?"

Ah, that explains the intensity.

The child scoffed and crossed their arms, "Is that even a question?"

Turning to Rivs, I saw a smirk developing on her face as she opened her wallet while still looking at the kid. "Now that's a kid that knows their shit."

Now I repaid the gentle hit on the arm to Rivs as she broke her concentration and looked at me in bewilderment.

"What?"

"I just don't think you should swear in front of a kid."

The kid piped in, "Nah, she's right. I know my shit."

My eyes widened to the kid and then to Rivs, who adjusted herself to also be crossing her arms. She and the 9-year-old Kool-Aid dealer looked identical in posture and grin for a split second.

"Yea, Dutch, the kid knows their shit." After her statement, she turned around and bought a small paper cup of red Kool-Aid for us both, then she noticed the kid playing with a pocket-sized bottle of bubbles with a wand.

"Hey, how much for the bubbles?"

I felt like I had to step in, "Rivs, please, I don't think-"

Rivs kept her focus on the bubbles, "Come on, every bubbles' got their price."

8

Unamious Swinging

"So, when's the last time you remember being on a swing?" I asked Dutch after we got a few comfortably silent pumps in. Our ambiance was only the creaking of the chains and my now sticky, soapy hands fumbling.

He made a few pondering sounds, "Honestly, I couldn't even make a wild guess."

I blew a victory bubble after finally getting the bottle open. I'm pretty sure that high-price, low-sugar Kool-Aid kid screwed the lid on extra mighty-kid tight. Just like they screwed me on the price. 5 bucks for an open bottle of bubbles. But I really can't be *that* upset. The kid's got a great business model already; immediate convenience and nostalgia.

"Do you think it was when you had that park friend? Or did you guys' mostly hang out on the monkey bars?"

Dutch looked over to me, sort of in astonishment, but it was mixed with something else I couldn't quite place. He sort of laughed under his breath.

"We did spend a significant amount of time on the monkey bars. I'm not entirely sure, though. That's not a bad guess. But in any case, I think I actually missed swinging."

Looking over at him, he wasn't looking at me or my direction. He was in his own swinging world, and isn't that what the chain links are all about? "Me too," I took my gaze off him, blew another bubble, and watched it float until it hitched a ride with the breeze. "I missed swinging too."

"I wonder what it is, the fascination of swinging yourself. If you think about it too deeply, it's kind of odd. Course, most of our human existence is probably based on strange events that we've come to normalize."

As I looked over at him, I could tell my eyes enlarged with excitement. "Well, hello Dutch!" I blew a few bubbles towards him. He amused me and let the bubbles completely land on him, and they softly popped on his face. What a good sport.

"I love that opening of discussion; let's unpack."

Dutch wasn't swinging very high yet. I think his mind was too deep in thought to divide some energy into the great art of pumping your legs.

"I don't know; humans can just be odd, like hugs, for example. We crave them from the right person; they're a source of comfort, acceptance, or fulfillment needed by someone in this world. But in theory, the whole concept of a hug it's just kind of comical yet adorable. Like I said, I don't know."

"Well," I stoically paused, mainly because that thought was so deep that I needed to search for a response to match it. "I was going to ask if *you* need a hug, but I think you got your fill of odd adorableness with the soft bubble attack."

Dutch chuckled, "Ah Rivs, always handy with the comedic relief. I appreciate that."

Glancing over at him, I felt I may have made him feel dumb or something for getting into a deep conversation, and I didn't want that. I, too, appreciated the deep depths of chit-chat.

"Although I gladly take the comedic reliever title, I think you're onto something in all seriousness. I don't really get hugs often. I'm not sure if a person, over time or whatever, can get the same chemical reactions by hugging themselves. There's gotta be a science behind that, or at least a trial."

"I mean, I'm sure it wouldn't hurt to give yourself a hug. It could be like a form of positive self-talk but in some sort of physical way. Or you could do both at the same time?"

The swing's chains jingled as I looked over at him in agreement.

"Now that's a pretty grand idea, I would feel a little silly at first, but with repetition and intention, I think that could have some positive effects."

I love how we were talking like fellow researchers, making a grand discovery at our lab that just so happened to be a local swing set. Hell, there are even refreshments available and bubbles if you're willing to pay the price! Perhaps there's been discoveries in stranger settings, I wouldn't doubt it, but I liked this brief relationship we were developing. Even if its lifespan is 24 hours. Speaking of which.

"So, we really have to do this jig for 24 hours? Is that super set-in-stone, or is there wiggle room?"

Feeling a slight shift in the vibe, Dutch stepped his feet back a little before swinging off again, catching some momentum. "I am pretty bothersome to be around, huh?" I could hear his sarcasm amongst the swings creaking.

An automatic eye roll rolled itself out, oops. "Not what I meant. I guess I'm just wondering."

"In the training I had, we were told the times given on the C.C.R. are strict and non-negotiable once they're agreed to, which we kind of did at your apartment." Dutch looked at me with a slight worry lingering in his eyes. "I don't mean to come off rude or bossy. I'm just-"

Placing my hand up, the hand that was holding the bubble wand, I kindly interrupted him. "Dutch, believe me, you haven't been the least bit rude; I honestly can't imagine you being rude unless someone really had it coming. We'll make good use of our time. I mean, it's gotta be for a reason, right?"

He gave me a nod while continuing to swing.

"Actually, earlier today, you said it best."

Dutch looked over with an eyebrow raised, "Come again?"

"You told me something like, we may have been meant to meet and help each other out. Like we were holding each other's compasses or something like that."

He looked like he was searching through his own transcripts, and the recall registered, "I do remember saying something like that, and I stand by it. Like I said, the thing with our birthdays, that's just too weird of detail to *not* be something."

Blowing an excitement bubble, I nodded in agreement. "Precisely! I was right on time, and you were running late. Sounds like it should have been the other way around, doesn't it?"

Getting a small laugh out of him, he slowed his swinging down. "Yea, maybe just a tad." Now he completely stopped and twisted the swing's chains, so he was facing me.

"I'm sorry I was late." He spoke in a whimsical, elegant way, like a line from a swooning scene of a decade-defining rom-com, but he was genuine. Dutch was always genuine.

Mirroring his swing sitting position, I replied softly, "Perhaps we were supposed to be born on the same day, but we were meant to meet at *this* exact time."

He looked a bit relieved, though I'm not sure why he would take responsibility for something totally out of his control.

"You weren't late; on the contrary, I think you made perfect timing."

His smile and posture remained the same, but I could tell some gears were turning in his head. "In this podcast, I heard awhile ago, they spoke about different love stories and timelines from famous movies, and dissecting them to uncover if fate is only movie based or if it can live within our reality,"

"Dutch, this is not a love story." I laughed, and thank goodness he laughed along with me.

"Yes, I believe we can both agree on that, but I'm wondering the same thing. If fate is an element that does in fact exist, or if it's fabricated."

Pondering for a moment, I thought of my reply after a few more bubbles. "I think it's a bit of both. Sure, fate weasels its way into lives for a good reason. But I also think people force things and call it fate to make themselves feel better. I don't know, that's a good question."

"Let's say hypothetically if you did believe in fate, with this incident aside, do you think you've encountered it? With love or something?"

"Nope." I made a fake throwing-up sound because I'm 10 years old, apparently. "Not everything is about some romantic love." And like the sassy 10-year-old I am, I blew more bubbles.

"I'll blow to that," Dutch stuck his hand out, indicating he wanted a turn with the bubbles, and I happily handed them right over. "Not everything is about some romantic love, such true words. Sometimes it's just about being present."

"Yes, and being a good human being."

Dutch blew another bubble I took as a sign of agreement, and all this fate talk had me thinking a little more inward than I had been before.

"So, before we became distracted by the wonderous essence that is Kool-Aid and what would come to be expensive bubbles, I mentioned baking to you."

"Ah yes, I did have a tab on that. I was wondering if that topic would circle itself back around. Or if you were, in fact, just curious about my potential as a baker."

"I mean, now I'm curious about both, but I actually did have a point I was trying to get at."

I turned my head slightly away for a moment, gathering my thoughts like they were well-composed but out-of-order papers.

"When making a big batch of cookies, you need a lot of flour. And typically, to make the process a little less messy, sometimes a recipe will instruct you to *fold in* the flour. That means you put one cup of flour in at a time, mix it with the other ingredients, and then add another cup until you're done."

Looking over to Dutch, I wanted to check if he followed along. Like the grand listener he is, he was right there in the trenches of my analogy.

"I guess I'm trying to explain that during this whole C.C.R., I've been folding it in. It isn't comfortable for me to talk about my deep issues and realizations, especially since I wasn't prepared for it and was in the midst of my isolation experiment. I wasn't expecting to talk to anyone in person for a while. This probably hasn't been the easiest for you, but I wanted to explain myself. And I'm ready to accept some guidance or whatever you've been trained to do."

Dutch took a breath, stood up from the swing, and I did the same. This felt like a profound moment, and I think we felt the same way. "Thank you, Rivs, thank you for folding it in."

"Still think we need to help each other, not just you helping me?"

With a bit of a sigh, a slightly silly sigh, he nodded. "Yepp, I believe I could get good use out of life with my compass back."
Dutch smiled, and I reflected it while gently taking the bubbles back into my possession so I had something to fidget with.

"I believe we have a night of planning and vulnerability ahead of us."

9

Rewound Compasses

October's air always had something particularly comforting floating about inside of it. Different from September's ode to new beginnings and exceptionally far from July's reckless endorphins. On the contrary, October's nippiness wisps were not cold in affection but provided a last hoorah of adventure before the seasonal trio *Frigid Chills* featuring November, December, and January began their grueling tour.

There's just something in how the sun still shines amongst the sky's decorated clouds. And the tree's leafy wardrobe change makes you feel like the month is working in your favor to do everything it can to slow down time. And for a while, I swear it kind of works.

Maybe it's the way the leaves fall or how festivities skyrocket once September has exited the stage, but even now, as Rivs and I walked back to her apartment, time couldn't have felt more pleasantly slow.

We exchanged the bubbles back and forth like two people sharing a paper bag with the contents of wine. And just as I'd imagine the wine would have gone in this scenario, if Rivs liked wine, we used up the bubbles until the last soapy drop. Just in time to meet the artistically collaged door once again.

Before retrieving her key, Rivs looked at me and broke our unestablished, but not uncomfortable, silence. Besides the words: *pass them bubbles here, my turn please,* and *ooOooOoo look at that one.*

"I'm kind of nervous," she revealed while putting the key in. "I want to create a game plan, for lack of a better phrase. But it's kind of weird and scary and intimidating." Her eyes were focused on the key, unturned and frozen in its purpose.

My eyes were also pressed to the picture, but then I turned them to the artwork on the door, and I remembered the scene she painted on her leg. And Rivs herself was the embodiment of a work of art in a human being if I had ever met one. She has so much potential, so much art to present and create, and I felt a small smile of determination come across my face.

"I truly believe the world would greatly benefit from the *Rivs Perspective*; I give you permission to trademark that. Adjusting to a new form of assistance isn't comfortable, to be honest. I mean, I wasn't expecting to open up to you either, and it isn't the comfiest. But I think we can do it together. Together, it may not be so bad."

After my ramblings had concluded, her fingers had turned. The apartment key must have radiated in its little brass ways, for its purpose was once again fulfilled. Without sounding too boastful, I believe Rivs and I deserved to find our paths in life that made us feel fulfilled in purpose as well.

Pocketing the key and opening the door, Rivs looked to me while presenting her arms out in an elegantly joking fashion to present her apartment entrance to me once more. "Together sounds nice."

After we both embraced the sentiment for a moment, we entered the apartment, and I felt the rush of her ambition begin. It was a new side of her, well, from the minimal sides of her I've seen. But I could tell that once she had a project in mind, she went into full dedication mode.

"Here," she had gone into a drawer immediately and thrown me a notebook that already had a pen tucked into the spiral wire.

"Pay no attention to my notes; just find the start of the blank pages. I know this is your job, but I have an idea." Rivs paused, and I realized she was waiting for some kind of body language from me to grant her permission to continue.

And I was bewildered at the thought of her needing any permission. But perhaps this is more of a respect thing, which is refreshing. I gave her an eager nod which resumed the gears in her mind.

"I think we should both privately journal for a little bit. I don't know about you, but it's easier for me to write what I'm feeling rather than speaking it off the top of my head. If I can think about it for a bit and write down what I want to work on and change, I think that will be of more use than sitting across from one another and forcing each other to speak."

"Say no more; I think that's an excellent idea."

She pulled another notebook out of a different drawer. I wondered if actual kitchen utensils were being housed in her kitchen or if it was just an extended storage space for her creativity.
"You're not patronizing me, are you?" She gave me a playfully but skillfully cocked eyebrow.

Her question caught me off guard and made me chuckle on impulse. "I would never dream of it."

That seemed good enough for her, "Good, well, let's get to the beginning stages of cleaning up our shit show lives."

While sitting on her couch, I now gave Rivs *my* signature furrowed eyebrow. Well, as of now, it's my signature. Feels pretty iconic. "Not a shit show."

"Hmm, a shit sitcom?"

"Wrong direction." I laughed as I could tell she would keep listing off different shit variations until I spoke something else in existence. "Our lives aren't shit shows, but they could use some guidance."

I looked over to Rivs to see she set up her journaling shop at her small kitchen table.

She was already in the deep depths of her intentional thoughts and penmanship. Flipping through the notebook, catching glimpses of words but not putting them together, I reached the valley of ink-free lined paper. But once I got it, I started to hit a wall.

What was *I* supposed to write? I was so focused on Rivs because that is my job right now that I wasn't even thinking about what I could possibly come up with for myself. Geez, perhaps that's part of my problem. I have never helped myself, and maybe I've set myself back because of it.

Journaling isn't particularly in my wheelhouse, but I like making lists. A hybrid would do; I can create what works for me. Maybe this activity is helping already.

- *I'd like to not feel like my chest will cave in if I'm not exactly on time somewhere.*

- *I've never been able to cut myself slack or reward myself for doing a good job. I think I expect too much from myself. Not sure why.*

- *I want to have a healthy relationship with eating.*

Writing that last point down made me feel shaky and cold for just a few seconds. I had to keep myself from looking around to see who saw me write that. It didn't feel real to admit it. It didn't feel really good at first, either. But since I've started, I don't want to leave it unfinished.

- *I want to be at peace with my body.*

- *I want to see the healthy version of my body.*

- *I want to know what it feels like to love every part of myself.*

- *I want to have true friends.*

- *I want to help myself and help others.*

I was writing so fast now; after that first vulnerable bullet point, the rest flew out so quickly. And I was crying, it was silent, but I felt the tears on my face. All of those thoughts felt locked away. But the amount of pressure that eased off from just simply *writing* them down was almost uneasy in itself.

Had I really been suppressing so much that I was crying in a stranger's living room? Rivs didn't really *feel* like a stranger, but she still kind of was in most ways.

As the thought of her peered in, I looked up across the room. She was practically nose deep in her notebook. She may have gotten the sense that someone was looking at her, for she popped her head up, and it appeared this was an emotional task for both of us.

"Finished?" Rivs simply asked, and I was so engaged in the activity that I didn't notice our setting had slightly changed.

The caramel candle was lit, and the room was a little dim. I really got lost in this world of spewing out hidden messages within me, not to notice a lighting change and a glorious scent. I should invest in some new candles.

Giving her a nod, she went over to the couch and sat on the other end. We both turned, resting our backs on the armrests, and our legs extended. At first, it felt a little weird, but following her lead felt a little less odd and more comfortable. I suppose we ought to get comfortable if we're sharing so deeply.

"We could swap notebooks if you'd like. Or we can read them out loud?"

The thought made me cringe so deeply that 7th grade Dutch had nothing on me. I wasn't exactly counting on reading each other's words, but I suppose that was part of the point.

"Dutch," She drew me back from my mind-circling. "I think we should just chill out for a little bit. Some self-care to give it a more professional tone. And I have a pretty stellar idea."

I released a deep breath, "Well, first off, thank you for bringing the word stellar back. And secondly, I didn't mean to seem so alarmed. I'm just a bit nervous. This is deep stuff."

"Ah yes, that it is indeed. And hell, I'm a bit nervous too. That's why I'd rather watch a banger like *Pride and Prejudice* for a while and feel more settled before we dive in deep again."

I'm sure she expected to get a goony sigh of relief and smile out of me, and if this satisfaction makes me predictable, I think I can live with that.

Rivs informed me of 4 things after I smiled in agreement with her movie proposal.

1. She would rent the movie; it was her pleasure.

2. I would need to help her hang the T.V. for viewing.

3. We will need our own throw blankets for the optimal viewing experience; she has a closet full of blankets to choose from.

4. There is a slight chance she may fall asleep, in which case it would be best to let her nap, and I may nap as well if I so choose. Unless that is against protocol. To which I did not know the answer.

All of that sounded fine and dandy; for the most part, I was a little taken back at the hanging of the T.V. request.

"If you go into the closet in my bedroom, and I give you permission to enter, there is a box cleverly labeled *T.V.* If you could please bring that in here, I'd appreciate it very much."

She stood up and began to make her way to the kitchen, prompting me to also get up and ask what she was up to.

"I am going to make you a cup of hot chocolate and myself a cup of

Kool-Aid." She smiled back at me. "Because we're worth the self-love,

damn it."

Replying with an inaudible laugh and nod, I navigated through

her artistical whimsical apartment to find her bedroom. Lo and behold,

it was a room with no door, but there was a beaded sort of curtain in its

place. Not entirely made of beads, but mostly. There were a few tiny

paper cranes scattered in there, each made with a different piece of

decorative patterned paper.

Moving past the beads, hearing their little chiming collaborative song, I

felt like I walked right into the creative mind that was generously mixing

me up a cup of hot chocolate right now.

Each wall was painted elaborately and entirely different than the others.

The first wall you see when entering the room has a dark fantasy tone.

There were mushrooms, like a dozen different types and colors, and large, dramatic trees that looked like they wanted to drape right off the wall.

The wall beside it carried the darkish theme but in an entirely different realm. It was like staring out of a window on a space expedition. There was something in the twinkle Rivs gave the stars and well-organized constellations that made the painting so enthralling. I felt much more attached to this piece than the constellations in the hallway, but both are incredibly well done.

For a moment, the painting threw me through a loop on the most prominent wall. I almost thought it wasn't a painting like I had been pleasantly fooled by Norman Rockwell himself. It looked like a giant gallery wall, full of framed pictures of various sizes. Some photos were of people, landscapes, and prints. But all of them were realistically painted.

My goodness, is she a talented creative soul. It's almost overwhelming to be in the presence of her talent, her personal space, and go back to her deep thoughts.

And on the wall housing the closet, Rivs wanted me to retrieve the box; it was painted with an assortment of leaves. This was arguably my favorite of the painted walls if I had to choose. I liked seeing all the different sorts of leaves; some even looked like they were in mid-fall.

After my admirable take of the room, I searched for the T.V. box. It wasn't a long search, Rivs closet had a few boxes in it and some out-of-packaging art supplies, but for the most part, it was pretty organized. Bracing myself for the heavy box, it was comically light. I wondered if she was pulling my leg, so I waited until I got to the living room to uncover the punchline.

"Alright, Rivs, either I am remarkably strong and am only now just

noticing, or there is a blank that needs filling."

Carrying a mug in each hand, she made her way to the living

room and laughed. "Allow me to fill it in for you." Setting our drinks on

the coffee table in front of the couch, where I rested the box as well, she

opened the folded cardboard flaps and pulled out a massive white sheet

and a Ziploc bag with tacks.

In realization, I laughed, then we laughed together; that felt

healing in itself. "So, when you said to hang the T.V., you literally meant

we have to hang it up."

I giggled again because even though I don't know Rivs completely, this is

the most Rivs thing ever.

"That is correct; I prefer to project my viewings. The art of

projection is lost." She started untangling the sheet after setting the tacks down. Once it was free, I took the opposite side and worked together to straighten it out.

"A while ago, I got rid of my T.V. I just didn't like the vibe it was giving off."

Once again, a very Rivs thing to say as I nodded like I could relate to her vibe insights. I felt terrible thinking about poking a hole in the wall that has her gorgeous meadow painting, but she pointed out where the tack holes already were, so my guilt was minimized a tad.

"Alright, wow, look at that dandy sheet. We did fantastically. Ready to host one of the best movies of our time."

She turned to me like we had both just spent hours forging something vastly complicated. A sly smirk represented what I imagined were sarcastic inner thoughts.

"That we did," Rivs gave me a pat on the back. "That we did, lad. Now for the throw blankets, I'll get my favorite one out of my room, and you can choose one out of the hallway closet."

Giving her a nod, we parted ways for our blanket retrieval expeditions. And my goodness, she was not exaggerating the number of blankets she had. It was literally jampacked. I was afraid I'd get 5 more with it if I pulled one out. Alas, this is not to say that I'm not impressed; this is a mighty collection and selection of blankets.

After the tremendous internal debate, I chose a blanket that, actually, come to think of it, reminded me of one of the walls in her room. The soft fabric was mainly black, and it was covered in a variety of watercolor-like planets and constellations.

I wonder what came first, the blanket or the mural.

Rivs blanket was a deep purple that looked extraordinarily fuzzy, the amount of fluff that would make a cloud envious. Just kidding, if clouds really were personified, I don't believe they would have envy. Or perhaps they envy the sky they lay on just a tad because it can remain where it is; it isn't forced to drift or disappear. Apparently, I have a lot of deep feelings about clouds. And this is another reason why I don't like letting my mind wander too deep; I'll get stuck.

Shaking my head to retreat from the cloud TedTalk formulating in my mind, I took a seat on the opposite end of the couch from Rivs. I laid the blanket on my lap and extended my legs onto the coffee table just as she was. With a couple of clicks and beeps, I saw the title screen pop up. I started feeling a kind of comfortable I hadn't felt in a while, maybe since childhood, with my parents. Had it really been that long? Goodness gracious, that's depressing. But what's not sad is the brilliance of this film and the connection it can bring to those watching it together.

So much, in fact, that the last scene I can remember admiring before my apparent sleepy crash was Lizzie and Mr. Darcy's dance. My favorite scene. I think my dream may have even had sprinkles of dramatic enemies to lovers' tones throughout. As my eyes slowly opened, I could hear the faint sounds of a sound asleep Rivs.

"Whelp, I guess that was my first sleeping on the job incident," I whispered out loud while pulling out my phone to check the time. It was a bit late. There was still some time on the C.C.R. left, and I also had a text message from my dad.

He was *sending over good vibes* and knew I was *doing a terrific job*.

Oh, dad, I can't lie. It did make me smile and give me a boost of confidence. Especially knowing that they most likely crafted the text together, carefully adding in dashes of cool lingo and encouragement but not an overbearing amount.

While typing my response, I hadn't noticed Rivs was waking up.

"Ah, texting *and* sleeping on the job, I see." She humorously accused, still cocooned in her fuzzy purple oasis.

"Guilty," I grinned and pocketed my phone after replying. "I actually feel pretty bad. I didn't mean to fall asleep; I'm sorry."

Rivs head tilted at me uncaringly, "Dutch, dude, it's fine. We may have actually fallen asleep around the same time. Sucked because I didn't get to see my favorite part. But apparently, I needed the rest."

My eyebrow lifted just a tad, having just been thinking a similar thought. "Oh really? What's your favorite part?"

A short breath exited before her reply, "Only the best part in the whole fricken masterpiece; when Mr. Darcy asks Lizzie to dance.

Finally." Her tone sounded like a personal sigh of relief, and I so got that.

I felt the giddy smile of like-minded movie scene admiration giggle across my goony face as I turned towards her. "No joke whatsoever, but that's my favorite scene as well."

"Well, yea, duh Dutch." She mimicked my body language. "We have good taste in cinema." Her grin was far more mischievous than mine, as always. "Whelp, good Sir, we've had our chill-out time."

I adjusted my posture to match the mood the room was bound to shift in. "Yes, you're absolutely right. I think that was a nice idea."

"Alright, save some of the mush. We got some deep diving feelings, move-making discussions, and plans to concoct." Rivs and the fuzzy blanket seamlessly moved in retrieving the notebooks and pens and beginning our next and almost final step in our C.C.R. time together.

"Would it be more painless if we swap notebooks and read to ourselves?"

With a quick thought, I nodded. "Perhaps that would be less difficult than reading our journaling deep inner thoughts aloud."

"Did you ever think your first day in the field would be like this?" Rivs chuckle sounded like it was partially out for the release of amusement but also on a mission to discover some hints of truth. To which I was more than happy to oblige.

"I didn't know what to expect. To be perfectly frank, I just wanted to ensure I did everything I could to help the human on the other end of the C.C.R. I will say, though, I wasn't expecting to be helped in return." There was a half-turned smile styled on my face. I felt it plaster faster than I could realize how I was feeling. I felt grateful and ready to embrace the vulnerability that would lead us onto better paths for a better version of ourselves.

With the swap of our notebooks, I swallowed the insecurities I had left

lingering in me, and I prepared myself to read Rivs inner thoughts.

10

The Planning of Plans

Geez, Dutch has been through some heavy shit. It makes me feel the tiniest bit lighter knowing what he's reading of mine. What if we both awkwardly look up at each other, dumbfounded, and we just call it a lifetime and never see each other again?

Well, granted, I know we're not intended to meet each other again after this interaction. But I don't know. There's something very intertwining about how we've already connected and opened up with one another. Even if we both live to be hella old, or one of us croaks before we see that dope thing we've been waiting to see, and we never see each other again, I'm still going to remember this goony fella. Maybe for the simple fact that I don't think anyone besides my mom has been so understanding and friendly to me. But also, for the fact that we just jive pretty well together.

Like we dabbled with before, I sincerely believe we were supposed to meet each other.

My ears perked with a tiny bit of attention at the soft sound of Dutch clearing his throat, which indicated that he was nervous about something.

"I hope it isn't too bad; I'm sorry if it is."

Looking up from his bullet points, which by the way, major penmanship points to Dutch, I should have given him a legend with mine so he could decipher my bullshit.

"Alright, well, let's make a mental note that you apologizing for things you shouldn't be apologizing about is one of the things we need to work on. Rest assured, there are worst things you could portray that we'd have to polish and refine; you could be super arrogant and full of yourself."

His grin was filled with relief and a joke I could see coming. "I mean," Dutch changed his body language to appear like his chest was sticking out more. "I have nothing to apologize for. My existence has been on the pedestal of perfection since my first diaper. And, I'll have you know, it was immaculate."

He hardly got his whole joke out without laughing at its own ridiculousness. Composing himself, he reverted to his Dutchly posture. "That was quite difficult to get through." An exceptionally short-lived laugh came out of him, as I could see the anxious apology that wanted to release from him.

"Some of those thoughts you've read, they're thoughts I've never said out loud, let alone had someone read them."

Letting out a sigh and slumping back, I nodded in understanding. "I can't say I feel the same way because our thoughts are different, but I get where you're coming from. I've never been one to open up about my inside stuff. And especially stuff to do with my mom."

Our eyes liberated themselves from the lined inscribed papers and to each other. I could feel the vibe of comfort and understanding lying over us like the blankets we were already wrapped up in. We trusted each other. We trust each other.

"You don't have anything to be sorry for. And please don't feel bad for saying sorry. I think I understand where that reflex comes from. But I want to say that I'm sorry, not for my personal actions but for the actions you've come across in your human experience. Whatever shit went down to bring up these thoughts, these bullet points you've made. They're not your fault." Nudging him lightly with my foot, a tear left his eye, and he promptly wiped it away.

"The things you've written here aren't your fault either. And thank you for those words. That was one of the most well-composed and kind things I've been told. And, goodness, I think I needed to hear that." Looking down in my notebook of thoughts, he appeared to reread some sections before looking back at me.

"I don't want to talk about your mom too much if that will upset you. I do think it would be valuable, and a part of my job, to sort of write out a plan of steps you can take once I'm gone. Does that sound okay to you?"

He was right, I didn't mind him reading my thoughts about going through that horribly dark period with my mom in the hospital and the animosity that had built up towards Indie, but I didn't feel like talking about it a whole lot. Although it did feel nice to get it all out and have someone read it. I took a pondering breath in and a settled breath out. "I will if you will." And I began to smile as he nudged me with his foot and brought it back to his comfy blanketed space.

"Without a question, we're in this together." Together we flipped our notebooks to fresh pages, much like the fresh start we're hoping to get out of this planning.

"What does the planning look like to you? I want to ensure we develop a structure that fits best with your vision."

That was a fair question. I tapped my fingers on the notebook in thought. "I'm recalled to my childhood," Putting my hands out in a theatrical manner and glancing over to Dutch as he took on the cue of a quizzical person in the deepest of thought and anticipating agony.

Letting the bit go with a laugh, I returned to a more serious tone.

"In school, we had a unit in English where we made 'I am' statements. Even though I was in elementary school, I can still remember how impactful and empowering creating those statements felt."

Cracking a smile, I was surprised with a montage of memories from mom's feminist gatherings at our old house.

"Those statements actually kind of remind me of my mom. I think she would have thought that was really cool." I could feel the nostalgia all over my face, and I silently regretted letting it in because sometimes it hurts to feel it go. But, I suppose it's better than not being visited by it at all.

Dutch nodded with an agreed smile. "That's brilliant; I really like that. And the wording of the statements is also like encapsulating a goal, a promise to yourself. I love it!"

Now I could see the Dutch, that loves to help people; he was getting fired up. It was nice to see, and I was suddenly feeling very honored to be his first C.C.R. though I still think the title is misleading for rock fans like myself.

"Maybe one of us can say our own statements out loud, and the other can write them down and give some feedback along the way?"

"Yes, that sounds productive and once again empowering. It's like when someone of importance back in the day just started rambling out loud and the person accompanying them panic searched for a pen and paper so they could write it all down." Dutch laughed in agreement, and I knew it was because he genuinely found it funny. And that felt more refreshing than I can express. With that, he also suggested that I go first.

"Alright, I'm going to keep this determined-positive-I-can-do-this attitude going." Hyping myself up, as I am used to with the whole solitude experiment. I took a moment to really think and understand what I wanted.

What do I want not only the next few days and weeks to look like, but what am I building towards for the years that lay before me?

Damn, this is deep. But it's necessary.

"I will cease my current state of excelled isolation and let the other party member know I am stopping."

Woah, actually, this whole talking-out-loud statement idea is already working wonders. That felt powerful as hell!

"That's a great place to start; I like that! In stopping your isolation thingy, what are you hoping to gain from it?"

Whelp that is a damn good question. And before I could untwist the knot in my stomach, I knew the answers. "Two things, actually."

Inside my mind, I began phrasing my statement.

"I am going to create an outstanding and revamped portfolio, and I will reach back out to Sofia Bianchi and step back into that path. Hell, maybe I can even arrange the same room with Georgia Sohn. She seemed pretty chill."

I waited until Dutch was done writing, and as he looked back at me, I began my following statement: a hard pill to swallow.

"I will compose a well-thought-out and open-minded message to send to Indie. I will begin a path of reconciling with my sister."

Dutch began writing the statement down without an initial comment. Towards the end of the jotting, he had a proud look. "That was a pretty big statement."

"Definitely wasn't easy to say, but I guess I kind of know it's true."

Setting the notebook in his lap, Dutch was currently the most comforting person I've encountered in a long time.

"We could compose the message together if you'd like; you don't have to do it alone."

I nodded before speaking, "Yes, please, I'd really like that."

Together, we formulated a message. And it suddenly hit me that Indie was the first to send a message because she unknowingly sent me Dutch. And as much as I'm not ready to say it out loud to myself or her, someday, I'll thank her.

I told Dutch I would like to send the message within the next week. I just wanted to let it all settle in and have a clear, level head before sending it out. To which, of course, he supported my decision, and I think we wrote a pretty good sister-reconcile message:

Hey Indie, I didn't close the door. I'm ready to work on opening ours back up.

I needed some space and time, and I did that for myself. Not to hurt you.

I'd like to start talking again. I'd like to get to know my sister again.

Love, Rivers

With a deep breath, I accepted and silently commended myself for the words I had dared to say out loud and the path I was beginning to forge.

I really needed this. This new perspective, direction, and someone to take the time and understand where I was coming from and going through. I needed Dutch, and now he needs me.

"I believe now, it's your turn. If you're feeling ready." I gave him a small but encouraging smile, something to help him ease into this exercise. Having attention on him and working through his dark issues isn't something he's used to, as I can tell.

"It might feel weird when you start talking, but honestly, just go with it. After that first statement, you'll feel what you saw on my face when I was making the statements. You got this."

With that reassuring pep talk, he started, and I got my pen ready to go.

"I am going to be patient with myself in working on not apologizing for things I shouldn't be apologizing for."

He was looking off somewhere else in the room while talking, but once he finished, he looked at me for validation he did it right.

"You remembered! And you kicked ass with that first statement, wasn't that inspiring?!"

Dutch started to loosen up a bit, "Yes, it was inspiring; I do like this feeling." He was a mixture of giddy and determined, ready to continue.

"I am going to say yes to more things and opportunities to get out of my comfort zone and gain more confidence."

My eyes widened as I wrote his words down; not in a bad way, that was a badass thing to say out loud. "Wow, wow, wow, Dutch, I really admire that! What do you propose you will gain from this? What do you want to accomplish?" I took some pointers from his responses when I said my statements; I believe he noticed.

With a deep and long inhale, his exhale was filled with his firm answer. "I am going to start attending a support group specifically for people living with an eating disorder and working on overcoming body dysmorphia."

His eyes were engaged with his hands. His thumb was pressed into the opposite palm, not hard it didn't appear, but perhaps that's what his hands did when his mind was a bit on edge.

"I've known about this support group for a while. I've even walked past the building while I knew a meeting was in session. I just, I never attended because then it would be real and roping other people into this darkly tangled jumble of hurt and repetition inside of me."

Dutch's thumb moved from his palm, and he gently brought his hands together and held them.

"But I think that's what has been missing. Recovering, understanding, and healing with others who have felt and seen similar horrors." There were a few seconds of heaviness in the air, to which Dutch intervened.

"Maybe I'll even make some friends," He lifted his head to me in a hopeful smile, and I reflected it back. "Or at least an accountability partner."

After I had written his words down, I set the notebook aside, and now I had a proud look on my face. "Well done, Dutch. Seriously, well done."

Pretending to take a bow, which made me laugh, he offered the same praise to me but in his own Dutchy way. "I don't think we could have done this so confidently and comfortably if we hadn't spent the day slowly opening up to one another. Or, as I have learned from an intelligent woman, *folding it in*."

We pointed at each other like two pals when an inside joke is perfectly sprinkled into a conversation. I began to wonder if what we had was friendship and if it would also be labeled as such. Or if what we had was merely connection, and whether or not that connection fades is entirely up to us. Either way, we both had someone who listened to us, and we had a new direction.

Unwrapping myself from the warmth of the blanket, folding it up, and Dutch following my lead, I was processing our time being over. How could hours feel like some other lifetime, and now we were being brought back to our respective timelines?

Randomly, I giggled a little as I remembered his story about the friend he made at the park. And now, though I don't know if he considers me a friend, he has the story of me.

"You seem to have an accidental habit of making brief but impactful friends, Dutch." Setting the folded blanket on the couch, I looked at him as he was doing the same but with a smirk of realization.

"You've got me there; it appears I do."

"But, from this point on, you'll make amazing lasting friendships that are super-duper."

He let out a huff of intimidation, "I am currently feeling for my future friends. Those are some big shoes to fill."

Waving his comment off in good humor, I formed a rebuttal in defense of his hypothetical someday friends. "Nah, don't worry, they can handle it."

Dutch was beaming for a second there, and then his face was painted with the inspiration of a sudden idea. "Oh!" He quickly grabbed the notebooks, handed me the one with his handwriting, and kept the one with mine.

"We have something else to add. Something that has helped us very much today that we should continue implementing in our lives."

I cocked my head a little, wondering what it could be.

"I will go for more walks." He stated and wrote down, then smiled back up at me.

Taking my pen and writing alongside his legible penmanship, I grinned and looked at him. "I will go for more walks."

Postlude

The Next Day in October

October's air remained crisp in its promises of festivities and last-minute outdoor excursions. Its minutes are collected by passing seconds, and its hours are harnessed by decisions within hours.

Dutch greeted his fathers at the door for their weekly dinner plans, a tradition longstanding throughout Dutch's young adult life and will stretch for years to come.

His parents had been whipping up some of Dutch's favorite dishes in celebration and eagerness to hear how the first day on the job was.

Slightly halted in their excitement, Dutch's parents noticeably became enticed as they both smirked at one another at the sight of their son. Seemingly beaming like he never had before. The ice was broken with a quick hug, and moving over to the kitchen.

"So, what's her name, son?" The one father spoke while taking a mischievous glance at their silently applauding partner, fully supporting this curious instigation.

Dutch skipped over the charade of playfully rolling his eyes; he embraced the extraordinary lingering feeling circulating throughout him. "Her name is Rivs."

The fathers tag-teamed on this embarkment of the inside scoop on their son's very otherwise private social life, "And when might you see this famous Rivs again?" Dutch's father asked as he finished pouring everyone a glass of wine and set Dutch's drink in front of him.

Dutch's hand gently grasped the glass and looked at the deep red contents before glancing at his anticipation-filled parents and finally fulfilling their wait.

"Never," he saw confusion quickly pool in their eyes where the thrill of

gossip had been occupying before. "I'll never see her again, but I'm fairly

certain she changed my life."